It's official. Margaret Anne Martin's perfect daughter Savannah has tied the knot with her unsuitable boyfriend Rafe Collier, and they're off on their honeymoon to sunny Florida, courtesy of Savannah's brother Dix and sister Catherine.

However, the happy couple barely has time to enjoy a night of nuptial bliss before they find themselves face to face with the dead body of their hostess, Frenetta Wallin, the next morning. And as soon as the local sheriff's deputy finds out about Rafe's criminal record, Savannah's new husband becomes suspect Numero Uno in what might not have been a natural death.

So much for a romantic honeymoon full of sun, sand, and hot sex.

Instead, Savannah must ferret out the truth about who wanted Frenetta dead, and why, before the sheriff can slap handcuffs on Rafe and slam the cell door behind him.

ALSO IN THIS SERIES:

BUSMAN'S HONEYMOON

Jenna Bennett

BUSMAN'S HONEYMOON
Savannah Martin Honeymoon Novella #10.5

Copyright © 2015 Bente Gallagher
All rights reserved.

Magpie Ink

ONE

"Do you," the minister asked me, "Savannah Jane, take Rafael to be your lawful wedded husband, to live together in marriage? Do you promise to love him, comfort him, honor and keep him for better or worse, for richer or poorer, in sickness and health, and forsaking all others, be faithful only to him so long as you both shall live?"

He paused so I could respond. I opened my mouth, but nothing came out.

It wasn't that I didn't want to marry Rafe. Quite the contrary. I wanted to, desperately.

But what if I failed? My first marriage had ended in divorce. I hadn't made Bradley happy. I hadn't loved him enough, or comforted or honored or kept him well enough. What if I couldn't keep Rafe happy, either?

I loved him so much it hurt. I wanted nothing more than to keep him for as long as I lived. But what if I lacked the wife-gene? We'd been doing well living in sin for the past six months. What if once we were married, things changed? What if getting married jinxed the lovely relationship we were building?

Rafe arched a brow, and behind me on the first row, my mother cleared her throat. There was a soft rustling going through the tent, as of a gentle breeze moving through dry grass. It was the sound of people starting to whisper.

Mother was probably hoping I'd say no. She'd allowed us to

get married here, on the grounds of the Martin Mansion, my ancestral home, in Sweetwater, Tennessee; an hour and a little more south of Nashville. She had even suggested it, and had arranged the occasion with her own hands, from the catered food to the dress I was wearing to the white gardenia in Rafe's lapel. But I don't think she'd have minded terribly if I'd changed my mind halfway through the ceremony.

The minister cleared his throat. He looked from me to Rafe and back. "Is there a problem?"

For a second, his gaze dropped to my stomach, round under the off-white silk and chiffon.

He probably thought we had to get married, as the euphemism goes. I was pregnant, visibly so. Maybe he thought I didn't really want to marry Rafe, and that I only did it because I didn't want to be a single mother.

And nothing could be further from the truth.

"No," I said. "No problem."

"Then..."

"I do." I looked at Rafe. "I want to be your wife. And I'll love you and keep you and be faithful to you for the rest of my life."

A corner of his mouth turned up, and his eyes warmed.

The minister turned to him. "And do you, Rafael, take Savannah to be your wedded wife, to live together in marriage?"

It might have been my imagination, but I could have sworn his voice had turned doubtful, as if he expected the answer to be no.

"Do you promise to love her, comfort her, honor and keep her for better or worse, for richer or poorer, in sickness and health, and forsaking all others, be faithful only to her so long as you both shall live?"

There was a pause. I imagined my mother holding her breath, and probably crossing her fingers.

"Yeah," Rafe said.

"You do?"

"Yeah." He nodded. "I do."

"Thank you." The minister sounded annoyed. "Do you have the rings?"

Rafe turned to David, who fumbled in his pocket.

David is Rafe's son, twelve years old, and up until about eight months ago, Rafe had no idea David existed. He'd been conceived during a one-night-stand in high school. Elspeth—David's mother—had never told Rafe she was pregnant, and after the birth, had been made to give the baby up for adoption. David had ended up with a lovely couple named Virginia and Sam Flannery, who couldn't possibly love him any more if he'd been their own. And none of us had known anything about any of this until Elspeth died last fall, and left everything she owned to her son.

And now David was standing as Rafe's best man at the wedding.

They were dressed in matching tuxedos, and looked great. Rafe, of course, is gorgeous, and I'm not just saying that because I love him. He has dark hair—what there is of it; he keeps it very short—dark eyes, and dusky skin. Eyelashes any woman with sense would sell her soul for, and a mouth that's made for kisses. The epitome of tall, dark, and handsome: six-three, with broad shoulders, long legs, and narrow hips.

And David looks a lot like Rafe did as a kid, with the same dark hair and eyes, and skin a shade or two lighter. Rafe's mother LaDonna was a blue-eyed blonde, and so was Elspeth. So am I, if it comes to that. The baby I was carrying would probably end up looking a lot like David.

He fumbled the rings out of his pocket and gave them to Rafe, who kept one and gave the other to me.

The rings were the one thing we had picked out ourselves. We should have gotten married a week ago, at a simple ceremony at the Nashville courthouse. But that plan got ruined when a sicko serial killer from Rafe's past took him captive and kept him from getting to the courthouse on time.

It's a long story. But it was after that, that Mother decided we should get married here, at the mansion, where she could control everything. She had paid for my wedding dress and Rafe's tuxedo, the flowers, the food, the tent, and the minister. But not the rings, since we'd already had those.

I looked at mine—or rather, Rafe's—lying in the palm of my hand. A perfect golden circle, with *Rafe & Savannah* and last week's date engraved inside.

"It's the wrong date," I told Rafe, fighting back an insane desire to giggle.

He shrugged. "We can fix'em later."

Not a chance. Once the ring was on my finger, I wasn't taking it off again. But if it didn't bother him, why should it bother me? The important thing was that we were almost married, and that every objection I made, made for a longer wait until I could peel his tuxedo off and have my way with him.

Pregnancy hormones. What can I say?

The minister gave me a stern look. "Put the ring on his finger and repeat after me: 'With this ring, I thee wed.'"

I took Rafe's hand with one of mine, and pushed the ring onto his finger with the other. It was hard, with the way my hands were shaking. This was it. This was really it.

The minister cleared his throat.

"Oh. Right." I looked up at Rafe. "With this ring, I thee wed."

He winked at me.

"Now you," the minister told him. "Put the ring on her finger, and repeat after me: 'With this ring, I thee wed.'"

Rafe's hands were not shaking, nor was his voice. And he didn't forget what to say, or forget to say anything. He positioned the ring at the tip of my finger, and then pushed it home while he looked into my eyes. "With this ring, I thee wed."

My breath went, of course, and my eyes filled with tears. My bottom lip quivered, and Rafe's curved. "Just hang on another minute," he told me.

I nodded, and tried to blink the tears away.

"I now pronounce you husband and wife," the minister said, oozing disapproval. I guess we weren't the kind of couple he liked to marry. He had probably expected better from Margaret Anne Martin's perfect younger daughter.

Nonetheless, he nodded to Rafe. "You may kiss the bride."

Rafe grinned. And looped an arm around my waist and yanked me up against him. And bent me back over his arm so I had to grab his shoulders so I wouldn't fall on my butt.

The tent gasped. Or not the tent itself, but everyone in it.

It was all for show, of course. He was laughing, his eyes dancing. But then he bent his head to kiss me, and those eyes turned darker, and the grin dropped off his face, leaving the kind of expression that could take my breath away, and frequently did.

I used to pass out when he kissed me. Literally pass out, to where I couldn't remember what had happened later. I've gotten more used to it lately, but my knees still turned weak, and my stomach swooped, and I clung to him while my head swam. It took a minute for the buzzing in my ears to translate into applause.

He was still laughing when he set me upright. "You all right, darlin'?"

"Fine," I said, holding on to his lapels so I wouldn't dribble into a puddle of love and lust at his feet. "Great."

He looked into my eyes. "I love you."

"I love you, too," I said. "It wasn't because of that. It's just..."

He's always had the ability to read my mind. I shouldn't have been surprised that he did it now, too. "You've been here before."

I nodded. "I couldn't keep Bradley happy. What if I can't keep you happy, either?"

"I've told you before, darlin'." His voice was easy. "I ain't Bradley."

No, he wasn't.

"We're going to be all right," I said.

He nodded.

"I love you."

He chuckled. "I know. You ready to do this?"

I nodded.

"Ladies and gentlemen," the minister raised his voice, "I'm happy... pleased... allow me to present to you Mr. and Mrs. Rafael Collier!"

I would have given him a dirty look, but I was too busy hanging on to Rafe's arm and smiling so hard my cheeks hurt while I practically skipped down the white runner that was the aisle up the middle of the tent. All our friends and acquaintances were applauding. Even Mother, in a ladylike, subdued fashion, and with a tight smile on her face. I made sure to direct an especially happy smile her way, but to be honest, I didn't really care that she disapproved. I had the man of my dreams, and he was mine forever, so what did it matter that Mother wasn't as happy for me as I was for myself? She wasn't the one who had to live with him.

Behind us, David offered his arm to Nashville homicide detective Tamara Grimaldi—my maid of honor—and they fell into formation behind us. Ginny and Sam beamed at their son as he came closer, and my brother Dix wasn't above giving Grimaldi a quick up-and-down look. They'd had something going on since my sister-in-law, Sheila, was murdered last fall. And no, I'm not suggesting that they've been carrying on an illicit affair while my brother's been in mourning. Of course not. But they've gone from being friendly to being something more, although I'm not really sure how much more there is. Dix clearly approved of the navy dress that outlined Grimaldi's athletic body, however. It was probably the first time he'd seen her in a dress. I know it was the first time I had. I was surprised Mother had managed to talk her into it. Literally and figuratively speaking.

Catherine and Jonathan, my sister and brother-in-law, were smiling and applauding, and so were the kids: three of theirs and two of Dix's.

Behind them, Mother's best friend Audrey had tears in her eyes, and my Aunt Regina, my father's sister, gave me a thumbs up. Aunt Regina happens to be the society reporter for the local newspaper, the *Sweetwater Recorder*, and I made a mental note to ask her whether Rafe's and my wedding had, or would, appear in the society column.

That would be one in the eye for our joint hometown, wouldn't it?

On the other side of the aisle, Rafe's boss at the TBI—the Tennessee Bureau of Investigations—was applauding along with Mrs. Jenkins, Rafe's grandmother. She was grinning from ear to ear, but I had no idea whether she actually understood what was going on. She's suffering from dementia, and some of the time she knows who Rafe is, but much of it, she thinks he's his father Tyrell, and I'm LaDonna Collier, pregnant with Rafe.

And now with the addition of David, the poor old dear must be more confused than ever. But she was here, and happy, so did it really matter what she understood beyond that?

And then we passed out of the tent into the sweltering June heat, under a bright blue sky, with fluffy clouds passing lazily overheard. In front of us, the Martin Mansion rose: two stories of red brick, with tall, white, Grecian pillars holding up the roof. A typical Southern plantation house: Tara, but red.

Or as Rafe has been known to call it, the mausoleum on the hill.

The long driveway was clogged with cars. The sheriff's truck, my brother Dix's SUV, my sister Catherine's minivan, Audrey's sleek Jaguar. Another truck, with a picture of the Virgin Mary in the back window, most likely belonged to José, one of the rookies Rafe and Wendell Craig were training for undercover work. He was inside the tent with a date. So were his fellow rookies: a black kid named Jamal, and white kid named Clayton. All three were around twenty years old; the same age Rafe had been when he'd been recruited by the TBI, straight out of Riverbend Penitentiary.

Eleven years ago. And to him, it probably seemed a lifetime.

It was a long time for me, too. Eleven years ago, I'd still had a year of high school to go, and was starting to go steady with my brother's best friend, Todd Satterfield. If anyone had told me than that I'd end up marrying Rafe Collier, I'm not sure whether I would have been insulted or thought it was a joke, but either way I wouldn't have believed it.

We reached the bottom of the wide steps up to the front porch of the mansion, just as an engine fired down on the road.

Rafe stepped in front of me. I stepped to the side so I could see. "Stop that. Unless you're wearing bulletproof armor under that tuxedo, you aren't any less mortal than me."

He scowled. "I just promised to keep you for the rest of my life. I ain't letting you get shot on your wedding day while I'm standing right next to you."

"And I'm not letting you get shot standing in front of me," I fired back. "I promised to keep you, too."

A dark SUV pulled out of the very bottom of the driveway and shot off down the street.

"Shit," Rafe said. "That's Satterfield." He glanced at me. "Ain't it?"

I nodded.

Todd Satterfield, my high school boyfriend and the man my mother wanted me to marry. The man who wanted to marry me, too. The man I had turned down so I could marry Rafe.

The rear of the SUV disappeared down the road in the direction of Sweetwater proper, and Rafe started breathing again, just as David and Grimaldi reached us. Behind them, Mother and Dix came out of the tent, followed by Wendell and Mrs. Jenkins. Everyone began moseying our way.

Grimaldi's brows were lowered. "Who was that?"

Rafe told her.

JENNA BENNETT | 13

"What was he doing here?"

"Prob'ly thinking he'd be Johnny-on-the-spot if Savannah decided to do a runner."

"Like in the movies?"

This was David, and I nodded. Grimaldi shook her head. "He obviously doesn't know you very well, if he thought you'd run away from your own wedding."

No, he doesn't. He knew the perfect Southern Belle I'd been brought up to be, and the girl I'd been before getting married the first time. But he didn't know—or understand—the woman I'd become since my marriage to Bradley fell apart.

The old Savannah, the one Todd knew, would never have gotten involved with Rafe. She'd have been too afraid of rocking the boat.

I owed Bradley a lot. And if I ever decided to go visit him in prison, I'd be sure to tell him so.

"What's going on?" Mother asked, a tiny wrinkle between her immaculate brows, as she and Dix reached us. Behind them, everyone else was filing out of the tent and coming toward us. "You have to get in position for the receiving line."

"We figured we'd just stand here on the steps and wave as people got in their cars and drove away," I said, although of course I knew the wedding wasn't over yet. There'd be several hours of eating and small-talk before we could go home and I could get Rafe out of the tuxedo and into bed. But I was feeling sort of giddy, and it was fun to watch Mother's face congeal.

"I'm afraid not, darling. You are to stand here and be polite until the last of the guests have moved past you and inside, and then you may come in for brunch."

"Yes, Mother," I said meekly, while off to the side, where Mother couldn't see him, Rafe grinned.

Until Mother turned in his direction. "Rafael."

I think he may have gulped. "Yes, Miz Martin?"

"I'll trust you to make sure Savannah behaves."

Rafe blinked. So did I. So, I'm sure, did Dix and Grimaldi. "Yes, ma'am."

Mother nodded regally, and swept past him up the stairs and through the double doors into the mansion. The better to terrorize the catering staff, I'm sure.

There was a moment's silence, before Dix said what we were all thinking. "What makes her think you can make Savannah behave?"

Actually, that wasn't what we'd been thinking at all. What I'd been thinking, was "*When did Mother start believing Rafe is better behaved than I am?*"

"I saw your mama naked last week," Rafe told Dix. "She's prob'ly afraid I'm gonna put the pictures on Facebook."

There was another pause. Then he said, "I'm kidding."

"Oh." Dix looked relieved.

"I did see your mama naked. But I didn't take pictures."

"I would hope not," I said, taking his arm. "People are coming. The three of you can go into the house. We'll hold the line here."

Grimaldi, Dix, and David escaped, and I turned to greet the first of the well-wishers.

TWO

It took an eternity—or felt like one—but three hours later, the wedding reception was winding down. I was counting the minutes until I could get out of my dress—and more importantly, get Rafe out of his tuxedo—when my sister Catherine pulled me aside into the kitchen.

"We booked you into a bed and breakfast for three nights," she told me, handing me an envelope. "On the Gulf Coast."

I took it, but said, "You shouldn't have."

"It seemed the least we could do," Catherine told me. "Mother took care of everything else."

And very ably, too. I shook my head. "No, I mean it. You shouldn't have."

"It's a nice place," Catherine said, sounding offended. "Jonathan and I took the kids there last year."

"I'm sure it is. But this is our honeymoon. What made you think we'd want to spend it in a house full of other people?"

She looked down at my stomach, round under the chiffon dress Mother had picked out. "It isn't like you didn't already indulge."

Well, no. But— "It's my wedding night! Surely you're not suggesting that I not have sex on my wedding night?" Rafe and I had spent last night apart, since Mother had insisted that the groom couldn't see the bride before the wedding. So I'd slept in my old room in the mansion, and Rafe had spent the night drinking beer with Dix on the other side of town. I'd been looking forward to the moment when I could get him naked and horizontal. Although I hadn't expected I'd have to drive to Florida before I could do it.

"If you start driving now," Catherine told me, "you can be there by ten."

The way Rafe drove, probably eight-thirty. Nine at the latest.

I sighed. "Fine. But don't say I didn't warn you. If we get kicked out for making too much noise, it'll be your fault."

"And my money down the drain," Catherine agreed, and handed me an overnight bag. "Have a good time."

"Where did you get this?" It was mine. The bag, I mean. Chances were the contents were mine, too.

"Your friend Tamara went to your house and packed for you," Catherine said.

Tamara Grimaldi had gifted Rafe and me fuzzy handcuffs and sexy underwear for Christmas. That knowledge made me wonder what she might have added to the bag, that she thought we could use for our honeymoon.

"That was thoughtful." Even if I would have preferred just to take my new husband home to Nashville and jump him in the privacy of our own bedroom.

"Have a good time," Catherine told me. She leaned in and kissed my cheek. "I'm so happy for you, Savannah. I'm glad you got to marry Rafe."

There was no 'got to' about it. Once I'd made up my mind that I was going to marry him, there wasn't anything anyone could do or say about it. But I'm sure she meant it sincerely. Unlike Mother, who had taken some time to warm up to Rafe—and who was only lukewarm now—Catherine had never seemed to have a problem with our relationship.

"I'm sure you'll be very happy together."

So was I. At least once we got back from the honeymoon and had some privacy again.

I glanced at the envelope in my hand. "It's a long drive to Florida. We should probably get started."

Catherine nodded. "Rafe's already in the car."

Of course he was. I'm sure he was more eager than I was to get out of there. Sweetwater isn't his favorite place in the world, and being in Sweetwater, in my mother's house, in a tuxedo, probably added insult to injury.

"Does he have a bag, too?"

Catherine nodded. "Your friend Tamara packed for him, as well."

The results of that should be interesting. Although I wasn't entirely sure how I felt about the mental image of the detective digging through my boyfriend's—husband's—underwear. Bad enough that she'd been digging through mine.

If wasn't as if the detective hadn't had her hands in worse places, of course. But still.

Although maybe she hadn't. Touched Rafe's underwear, I mean. Maybe he'd have to go commando for the next three days, and didn't realize it yet.

I grinned. "This should be interesting."

"Then go," my sister told me. "Don't leave him waiting."

No. The sooner I got him to Florida and into the B and B, the sooner I could investigate the contents of the bags Grimaldi had packed.

I skipped out the door, still in my wedding dress, bag in hand.

Rafe was indeed waiting at the foot of the stairs, leaning against the car, and he was still wearing his tuxedo. Or at least wearing the necessary parts of it. He'd taken off the jacket and the bowtie, and had unbuttoned a couple of buttons and rolled up the sleeves of the shirt halfway to the elbow.

When I opened the front doors and ran down the stairs, he grinned. "Ready to blow this joint?"

"More than ready." I handed him my bag, and he tossed it in

the trunk next to his own before slamming the lid.

"Then let's go. It's a long drive."

Someone must have told him the good news, then. Probably Dix and Grimaldi.

"I'm sorry," I said. "It wasn't my idea."

He glanced at me, in the process of sliding behind the wheel of the Volvo. "What wasn't?"

"The bed and breakfast." I pulled the seatbelt across my chest and fastened it, as Rafe turned the key in the ignition. "I think it was probably Catherine's idea. She and Jonathan have three kids. They're used to having sex in a house full of people."

Rafe nodded and shifted the gears. We rolled off down the driveway. As we picked up speed, an awful banging and clanging came from behind us.

I glanced over my shoulder. "What's that awful racket?"

"Cans," Rafe said. "Your brother told me his kids and your sister's kids have been collecting soda cans for the past week. They're all tied to the back of your car."

"You're kidding." I glanced out the back window again, where a small cloud of dust floated. Occasionally, I got a flash or red from a Coke can or a flash of green from something that was either Seven-Up or Mountain Dew.

I turned back to Rafe. "What about the smears on the window?"

"Those ain't smears," Rafe said. "The kids wrote *Just Married* on the back window with white shoe polish."

I blinked at him, dismayed. "It'll come off, right?"

I couldn't drive around Nashville with *Just Married* scrawled across my car.

He shrugged. "I hope. I ain't been married before, so this is all new to me. Did it come offa yours and Bradley's window?"

"Bradley rented a convertible," I said. "No windows."

Rafe nodded. "As soon as we get outta sight, I'm gonna pull over and take the cans off. I ain't driving to Florida dragging a hundred soda cans behind me."

No, I wasn't either. However— "I'm afraid we'll have to wait a bit longer than just until we're out of sight of the mansion. I'm sure everyone in Sweetwater knows we were getting married today. I asked Aunt Regina, and she said she'd put it in the paper. If we stop and take the cans off while we're still within the town limits, somebody's sure to tell my mother."

Rafe sighed, but didn't argue.

"Luckily it's a small town," I said brightly.

"Not small enough," Rafe muttered. But he waited until we were out of town and ready to turn onto the interstate before he pulled off into a gas station and stopped the car. "Might as well fill up the tank. We got a ways to go."

I nodded. "I'll untie the cans."

Rafe went to deal with the gas while I walked around to the back of the car and squatted, careful not to trail the bottom of my off-white chiffon skirt in the dirt.

There were a lot of cans. Maybe not the hundred Rafe had guessed—the kids likely hadn't had time to gather that many in the past week—but plenty. Coke and Seven Up, Dr. Pepper and Mountain Dew. A few Michelob and Miller Lites I figured must have come from Rafe's and Dix's bachelor party last night. Or maybe Catherine and Jonathan sat around at night after the kids were in bed, drinking beer.

Each and every can was tied to the back of the Volvo with an off-white satin ribbon looped through the tab on top of the can and tied in a bow. It took forever to untie them all, but I felt too guilty about the children's efforts in collecting and tying to cut all the ribbons and toss the cans in the nearest trash can. Instead, I untied them all and told Rafe, "Pop the trunk."

He did, and I tossed them in there, where the ribbons draped over our two overnight bags and the spare tire. "There." I slammed the trunk lid down again and leaned in to pick at the white letters scrawled across the back window. I'd hoped the white substance would just flake off, like chalk, but no such luck: instead, it stuck to the underside of my fingernail like glue. I left it alone and got back into the car picking at my French manicure. Rafe followed a minute later, and then we were off, headed south on Interstate 65 bound for the Gulf of Mexico, thankfully without the racket of bouncing tin cans as accompaniment.

We stopped once for a quick dinner—somewhere just south of Montgomery, Alabama—and got a round of applause when we walked into the restaurant. I guess Rafe's pared-down tux and my wedding dress were a dead giveaway what we'd been doing today. Or maybe it was the shoe polish on the car.

Then we got back into the Volvo and kept driving. I turned out to be right. It was well past eight-thirty but not quite nine o'clock when we pulled into the parking lot beside the Davenport Inn B and B in Davenport, Florida.

Or rather, it was not quite nine o'clock in Sweetwater, Tennessee. What my sister had neglected to mention, was that Davenport was on Eastern time, not Central, so we'd not only had to drive for seven hours to get there, we'd lost an hour along the way, too, when we crossed the time line.

So really, Catherine was right. It was almost ten.

"But we're here now," Rafe said, opening his car door and swinging his legs out. I followed suit, and watched as he lifted his arms above his head to stretch out the kinks from the last half a day. The bottom of the tuxedo shirt escaped from the waistband of the black pants and rode up to expose a strip of taut, dusky skin.

I swallowed, and tried to hide it by clearing my throat. "I can hear the ocean. But I can't see it."

Rafe lowered his arms and shook his head. "You wanna go see if we can find it?"

Given how big it is—even if we were only talking about the Gulf of Mexico and not the entire Atlantic—I didn't think we'd have any problems. However— "We won't be able to see much. It's dark. And late. We should probably make sure we can get in."

Rafe nodded and turned toward the house, but I thought he looked disappointed.

"Although I guess ten minutes one way or the other won't make much difference. Sure. Let's go see."

He smiled, which made tramping around an unfamiliar town in the dark looking for the beach in my wedding dress and high heeled sandals totally worth it. When he reached for my hand, I put it in his and fell in beside him as he headed in the direction of the waves.

"I guess you must really like the ocean?"

He glanced down at me. "I never spent much time on the beach. We never went on vacation or nothing, growing up."

I nodded. Rafe's mother LaDonna had been all of fifteen when he was born. A single mother, still living with her own mother and father. Wanda died within a few years, and after that, it was Rafe, LaDonna, and Old Jim, who had nothing but contempt for his only daughter, and less than that for the kid she'd spawned.

No, it hadn't been an idyllic childhood. I wasn't surprised that beach vacations hadn't featured large.

"We went a couple of times," I told him. "Usually to Orange Beach, in Alabama."

He nodded, and I added, "You have seen the ocean, haven't you?" This wouldn't be his first time, would it? Because if so, the experience would be so much better in daylight, when he could actually see the sea.

He smiled, his hand warm around mine. "Yeah. The summer after I graduated from high school, and before I got myself thrown in prison, I got a job in Birmingham."

"Working on cars."

He nodded. "A couple of the guys drove down to the Gulf one weekend, just to see what it was all about. Had some shrimp, drank some beer, picked up some girls."

"I didn't need to know that last part," I told him.

He shrugged, unrepentantly. "I never pretended I was a monk, darlin'."

No, he hadn't. "So what did you think?"

"About the water? Pretty color. Big."

I tilted my head to look at him. It was hard, in the dark out here. It was cloudy, and Davenport didn't seem to believe in street lights. Rafe's expression was hard to make out. "You know how to swim, right?"

He chuckled. "Sure. I grew up next to the river."

So he had. The same tributary of the Duck River where Old Jim had drowned the year Rafe was twelve.

"Good," I said. "That way I won't worry about you drowning."

"You wouldn't have to worry about that anyway, darlin'. I like looking at it, but I don't like going in too deep. You never know when a shark might could come along and decide to take a bite."

A weakness. And here I hadn't realized he had any.

"Are you afraid of sharks?"

"Isn't everybody?" Rafe asked. He stopped. "There it is."

There it was. Big and black and noisy, with white-capped waves.

We stood in silence for a moment, listening to the water crash against the shore.

"OK," Rafe said. "You were right."

I glanced at him and he added, "It's late and dark. We can look at it tomorrow. When there's something to see."

I didn't tell him I'd told him so. Just turned around and trudged back toward the B and B on my strappy sandals, holding the bottom of my wedding dress up off the ground.

Two minutes later, we were back in the parking lot behind the B and B, dragging our overnight bags out from under the satin ribbons and cans, and making our careful way across the gravel—

or maybe it was crushed shells—toward the back door. It was dark out here. You'd have thought the owner of a B and B would make sure the parking lot had decent lighting, but no. Everything was pitch black. The light above the back door wasn't even lit. I could hear the rolling of the waves in the distance, and closer at hand, the buzzing of insects. Maybe that was why the lights were off. If the lights were on, the insects would probably be dive-bombing the bulb. And Florida insects are large. It would be like being hit in the head with a wedding bouquet.

We hadn't had a bouquet toss back at the mansion. Nor the traditional garter ceremony, in which Rafe was required to pull the garter off my leg with his teeth. My mother is much too refined to allow that kind of ribaldry in her home. She had planned a tasteful wedding ceremony, and a tasteful—and tasty—reception afterwards, and Rafe and I had been given the heave-ho before things had wound down all the way. So the wedding bouquet was somewhere in the mansion. Hopefully someone had picked it up and would do something with it. I'm not sure gardenias dry well, but it was worth a try. Maybe I'd call Mother and ask her to hang it upside-down from a rafter in the old slave cabin, to see what would happen to it.

But I digress. We made our way to the back door, where Rafe nodded to the door. "My hands are full. Try the knob."

I tried the knob. It wouldn't turn. "Uh-oh." I glanced at him. The idea of spending our wedding night on the beach didn't appeal at all. It might sound romantic, but I was willing to bet it would just be uncomfortable.

In the distance, thunder rumbled, as if it agreed with me.

"Knock," Rafe said. "It's only ten. Not like they'll be asleep."

Hopefully not. "There's a bell." I used it, and heard the sound reverberate through the house.

We waited.

Nothing happened.

I rang again.

We waited some more.

"Shit," Rafe said.

I reached up to my fancy coiffure and pulled out a hair pin. "Why don't you just unlock it?"

He gave me a look.

"You've done it before," I said.

"On storage units and empty houses," Rafe answered. "Not somewhere where somebody lives. This'd be criminal trespass."

"Surely not. We have a reservation." I wiggled the envelope Catherine had given me.

"I don't care," Rafe said. "I ain't spending my wedding night in jail. Ring the bell again."

I pouted, but rang the bell again. And leaned on it, for good measure. The shrill tone echoed through the house, shaking the windows and rattling my teeth.

Two minutes later, a dark figure came stomping through the house, headed for the back door. I could see the smoke coming out of its ears even before I could determine whether it was male or female.

It yanked open the back door, and we found ourselves face to face with a woman around thirty, with lots of fluffy, platinum blond hair, a heavy tan, and an attitude. "What the hell's the matter with you? There are people in here trying to sleep, you know!"

She looked from me, directly in front of the door, to Rafe, behind me, and her expression changed. "Oh. Hello!"

They always do. Expressions, I mean. Women get a good look at my boyfriend—my husband—and they start acting like teenagers.

I smiled. With lots of teeth. "Hello. My husband and I have a reservation for tonight." I made sure to put heavy emphasis on the word 'husband.' "Are you—" I consulted the information Catherine had given me, "Frenetta Wallin?"

She tossed hair the consistency of cotton candy over her

JENNA BENNETT | 25

shoulder. "Do I look like my name would be Frenetta Wallin?"

"I have no idea," I said. I mean, parents name their children strange things sometimes. I'd gone to high school with a girl named Epiphany. And if Frenetta was a family name...

The woman sniffed. "Frenetta runs this place. I'm just one of the guests. My boyfriend and I were busy when you rang."

"Sorry to get you out of bed," I said politely, since the way she'd pronounced 'busy' left no doubt what they'd been doing. The same thing Rafe and I would be doing a few minutes after we got to our room. "We'll just get ourselves situated if we can't find Frenetta."

She tossed her hair again. "Three of the rooms upstairs are occupied. We're in number 1. Number 3 is across the hall, and there are two women in there. And an old couple is in number 4. Number 2 is empty."

Then number 2 must be meant for us.

"Thank you," I said. "I'm sure we'll figure it out."

"Breakfast from eight to ten. This morning was waffles."

So tomorrow would probably be something else.

"I'm sure whatever it is will be fine," I said. I was pregnant, so I didn't really care what I ate as long as there was plenty of it. And two years of prison food had taught Rafe not to be picky.

Not that I imagined he'd been used to *haute cuisine* before that, either. The Colliers' diet had probably been pretty simple, too, between LaDonna, Old Jim, and the lack of money.

The woman shrugged. Her breasts jiggled under the loose T-shirt. "Suit yourselves. Frenetta is probably asleep. She's, like, ancient."

"I'm sure we'll figure it out. Thanks for coming down to open the door."

She finally took the hint and moved out of the doorway so Rafe and I could get into the house. Rafe locked the door behind him.

"I'm going back upstairs," our new friend said. "I guess I'll see you tomorrow. If you stick around."

She walked away, leaving Rafe and me to stare at one another. He arched a brow.

"What does she imagine we'll do?" I demanded. "We have a reservation!"

He shrugged. I looked around. "I guess maybe we should try to find Frenetta."

"If she's in bed, I ain't walking in on her."

Well, no. I guess I didn't really want to do that, either.

"Like you keep saying, we got a reservation. And there's an empty room upstairs. I vote we go on up there and get comfortable."

There was a lot to be said for that approach. Even though it felt sort of weird, making ourselves comfortable in a house where the owner didn't know we'd arrived.

"It *is* kind of late, I guess..."

"And our wedding night," Rafe reminded me, with another wiggle of his eyebrows. Both of them this time.

"Right..."

He shook his head. "Those good manners are gonna be the death of you one of these days, darlin'. C'mon." He scooped me up—bags and all—and headed in the direction our fellow guest had disappeared.

I squeaked, but didn't bother to tell him I was too heavy. It was obvious I wasn't. He was carrying me, with baby onboard, and both bags through the house as if we weighed nothing at all.

However, it was just a week since he'd been injured.

"Are you sure you should be doing this?"

"I'm fine," Rafe told me, not even out of breath. "You can see for yourself once we get upstairs."

I intended to, and told him so. And then I let him focus his efforts on climbing the stairs, since in spite of his assertions to the contrary, I wasn't at all sure he was fine.

THREE

The stairs came up in the middle of the house, and we found ourselves on a landing surrounded by four doors. They were numbered from 1 to 4, with number 1 behind us on the right, and numbers 3 and 4 to the left. Everything on that side of the house was quiet, but from behind door number 1 came the sound of bedsprings squeaking and what sounded like a couple of piglets grunting and squealing. Since there was unlikely to be piglets inside the house, it was probably just our new friend and her significant other going at it.

"Didn't waste any time," Rafe said softly.

I shook my head, trying to keep a straight face but failing miserably. "We don't sound like that, do we?"

"I don't," Rafe said. "You..."

"That's awful!"

He grinned, white teeth flashing in the darkness, and I added suspiciously, "You're joking, aren't you? It's a joke, right?"

"Yes, darlin'. You don't sound like a dying frog when you come." He stopped in front of the door to number 2 long enough to let me reach down and turn the knob. "You're not so much a moaner as a screamer."

"Am not!" Making that kind of noise in that situation—especially where other people could hear—was unladylike.

"Sure you are." He nudged the door wider with his foot and

carried me across the threshold. "I'll do a better job of this when we get home. When I don't have both you and the bags to deal with."

I knew it. "I'm too heavy."

"You're not too heavy." He kicked the door closed behind him. "The bags are too heavy."

The bags were not too heavy. "I'm fat."

"You're pregnant," Rafe said. "And my arm had a knife go through it a week ago. Now shut up before I drop you."

"You wouldn't drop me."

"Watch me." He let go of my legs, and I squealed—but not like a dying frog, or for that matter a piglet—and dropped both bags to hang on to him. He chuckled, and lowered the rest of me gently to stand in front of him.

The next minute or two were nice and peaceful. Just Rafe's arms around me, and Rafe's mouth on mine: the scent and taste and feel of him. I was getting nice and relaxed and turned on, which isn't a bad thing on your wedding night.

Until something banged hard against the wall and kept banging.

I buried my face in Rafe's shoulder. My cheeks were hot, but I'm not sure whether it was embarrassment or humor.

Rafe had no such problem. He was shaking with quiet laughter.

"This is awful," I told his shoulder.

His voice was uneven. "Gimme two more minutes, and that'll be you and me."

"Over my dead body!" I was not providing prurient entertainment for the people in the room next door.

"And here I thought you couldn't get enough of me."

"I can't get enough of you," I told him. "I just don't want the people next door to talk about us the way we're talking about them."

"I don't care if they're talking about us," Rafe told me. "I just wanna make love to my wife."

How could anyone possibly fail to melt? I felt myself going all gooey inside, and not just in the sexual way.

However— "Can you do it quietly?"

"*I* can." With emphasis on the pronoun. "Not sure about you."

I sniffed. "I'm a lady."

"Not in bed," Rafe said. And added, "Thank God."

OK, then.

"And anyway, you're married to me now. I think your status got revoked."

"Thank God," I said.

He grinned. "No regrets?"

I shook my head. "Not a one. I'd marry you again tomorrow." And the next day. And the day after that. And ten years from now. And twenty.

"It ain't just cause I knocked you up?"

"No." How could he even suggest that? "I love you. I'd marry you if I weren't pregnant, too."

"Good to know."

I tilted my head to look up at him. "You weren't really worried about that, were you?"

"It crossed my mind."

I shook my head. "No. I married you because I love you. I want to have your children. But I would have married you anyway."

He nodded, but didn't say anything. After a second I added, "For the record, you didn't propose just because you knocked me up, did you?"

"No," Rafe said. "I woulda married you if you weren't pregnant, too. But I guess it made it a little easier to ask."

Why on earth?

"Less chance you'd turn me down. I figured if you were having my baby, you'd have incentive to say yes."

"So we were only having so much sex so I could get pregnant so you could make sure I wouldn't say no when you proposed?"

"No," Rafe said. "We were having sex so you could get pregnant so I could make sure you'd say yes when I proposed so we could have more sex."

"So it's all about the sex?"

"Course." He grinned. "I'm a man. It's all we think about."

"Good." I grinned back. "Because I've spent most of the day planning how to get you out of the monkey suit."

"Yeah?"

"Sure. That's why I kept forgetting my lines. I was thinking about you naked." I reached out and started flipping his shirt buttons open.

He stood there and let me do it, but he sounded shocked. And maybe a bit intrigued. "You're kidding."

"No." The last button gave way, and the shirt fell open. I reached up to brush it from his shoulders. "You look good in a tuxedo. But you look better like this."

I bent my head to drop a kiss on his chest, although I have to admit that running my palms across his skin had just as much to do with making sure none of his wounds had opened back up again as with pleasure. It was just a week ago that some maniac had used him for whittling practice, and the scars were still pink, and—from his quick inhalation—sensitive.

"Just making sure you're all right," I murmured.

"I'm fine." If a little breathless. Hard to tell whether it was from pain or something else.

"Yes," I agreed, "you are."

He chuckled. "For the record, I've been thinking about how to get you outta that dress, too."

"Really?" That was gratifying. "The simplest way is to ask."

"Yeah?"

"Sure." I turned my back to him. "There's a zipper."

He took a step closer. "Not exactly playing hard to get, are you?"

"What's the point? I married you. You paid for the cow." I waited for him to find the zipper and pull it down. The rasp of tiny teeth was loud in the quiet room. Next door, the bed made a final convulsive bang against the wall and subsided, quivering. We heard simultaneous gasps.

"The walls must be made of cardboard," Rafe muttered, as I shrugged the dress off my shoulders and let it drop to the floor. He reached out a hand to help me step out of the cloud of frothy chiffon, and added, when I turned to him, "Oh, yeah."

The underwear. "My mother has good taste," I said demurely.

"If you don't mind," Rafe answered, "I don't wanna think about your mother right now."

Come to think of it, I didn't either. "Sorry. But she put together a lovely wedding for us."

Rafe nodded. "I'm just waiting for the other shoe to drop."

"I thought you liked it when I kept them on."

"Not the kind of shoes I was thinking of. But I do." He took a step back and looked me up and down. Strappy sandals, skimpy lingerie, and round stomach. I resisted the temptation to cover the bulge with my hands, and when his eyes came back to meet mine, I was glad I had.

"Mine," he told me.

I nodded, my heart beating faster. "All yours." Every inch. Including the extra-large stomach.

"Everything OK in here?" He reached out and put his palm flat against the side of it. His hand was warm and hard, while the air conditioning pumping from the vents was cold.

I nodded. "I think he's asleep. Or she." At four months along, I had started to feel occasional flutters when the baby was awake and moving around inside me, but I still didn't know whether it was a boy or a girl.

"You mind if we wake her up?" His arm glided around to my back to pull me closer. The lace of my bra pressed against the heat of his skin, and the satin of my panties slipped across the worsted of his pants with a whisper of sound. My stomach poked his.

"Not as long as we're quiet." The occupants of the room next door were showing signs of life. I could make out voices and hear the squeaking of bedsprings. Hopefully it was pillow talk and they were settling down for the night instead of gearing up for another round.

"You just worry about yourself," Rafe told me, with a nudge toward the bed. "Although it ain't much of a wedding night unless there's a little blood and someone screaming."

"You've been in law enforcement too long."

"That ain't the kind of screaming I was thinking of, darlin'."

We reached the bed, and stopped. I'm not sure why things were so awkward, since we'd been sleeping together for months now without any awkwardness at all.

And Rafe must be thinking the same thing, because he looked sheepish. "I didn't figure it'd be like this."

I shook my head. "I thought we'd drive back to Nashville and be in our own bedroom by sundown." Familiar. Comfortable. With nobody banging like hammers on the other side of the wall.

His smile turned genuine. Or maybe 'cocky' would be a better word. "Bet I can make you forget where you are."

I bet he could, too. And part of me wanted him to. The other part was still convinced I had to be ladylike and quiet so the neighbors wouldn't guess what was going on.

Rafe took a step closer to me. His voice turned low and seductive. "Mrs. Collier."

I gulped. Other than the preacher, and the toasts during the reception, this was the first time anyone had called me that. And it was amazingly effective. I felt my knees weaken. Or maybe that was just because of the look in his eyes.

He leaned closer. My breath hitched and my eyes went out of focus. When he reached out and gave me a push, my knees buckled and my butt hit the bed.

He followed me down, and for several minutes, nobody said a word. He was as good as his word: by the time he stopped kissing me, I'd forgotten all about where I was. And when I looked around and realized it—Florida; people on the other side of the wall—I couldn't care less.

"Don't stop."

"I wasn't planning to," Rafe told me, fumbling for his zipper. "Dunno if I could if I tried."

I didn't believe that for a minute. He had absolute control over himself. If I told him to stop, he'd stop, no matter where he was or what he was in the middle of doing.

But in this case I didn't want him to. I waited, twitching with impatience, for him to shimmy out of the tuxedo pants and underwear and come back to me. And when he did, I wrapped my arms around his neck and held on.

Things went on in this vein for a while, with touching and kissing and stroking and petting. I wasn't fully cognizant of what was going on around me, I have to admit. I was too focused on what I was feeling to really pay much attention to what was going on. I was busy processing how it made me feel.

Good, in case you wondered.

He was careful not to lean too hard on my stomach, but other than that, it was business as usual. When Rafe touches me, I pretty much forget everything else.

Until he shifted between my legs, and thrust.

I must have made a sound then, because his hand came up to cover my mouth.

"Shhhh!" he whispered. "Be vewy, vewy quiet."

In Elmer Fudd's voice.

I laughed, of course. He grinned back. And then he moved. And my laughter turned to a moan—not a particularly quiet one—and after that, I didn't really care who was in the next room or how thin the walls were or what they could hear.

I woke up the way I usually do, curled up on my side spoon fashion, with Rafe's arm around me, his hand splayed on my stomach, and his nose buried in my hair. He was breathing slowly and evenly, his respirations tickling the fine hairs at the nape of my neck.

We had forgotten to close the drapes last night, so bright sunshine was pouring into the room. I looked around, while taking care not to move too much. Rafe sounded like he was sleeping, and he'd had a big day yesterday, between the wedding, driving to Florida, and what we'd spent half the night doing. I figured I should let him sleep. But since I hadn't really seen the room when we arrived, I wanted to take a look now.

It was a pretty good size. About the same as our room in Mrs. Jenkins's house at home. They were both Victorian houses, built within a few years of one another, and the bedrooms are usually pretty generous. Not the size of master bedrooms in the McMansions they build these days, but bigger than in houses that were built during the middle part of the twentieth century.

It was nicely decorated, in a sort of tropical/Victorian/old lady blend. The walls were bright yellow, and most of the furniture was white wicker. The chairs all had doilies on the arms. Tropical turquoise doilies. The bed was a four-poster with drapes—or perhaps it was mosquito netting—dragging the floor. Sort of romantic—unless you thought too hard about the Florida bugs. The sheets were tan—probably because they were easier to keep clean than white—while the comforter was striped. A big, ornate mirror hung above the low dresser on the other side of the room, its frame covered with shells. And the top of the dresser was home to an eclectic mix of stuff. A bowl of shells rubbed elbows with an old-fashioned boxy TV and a stuffed bird, while a row of colorful paperbacks stood upright between two starfish bookends. By squinting, I could read the titles on the spines, and recognized one of my favorites: *Tryst in Tartan* by Barbara Botticelli, better known—at least to me—as Elspeth Caulfield,

David's mother and the girl who had taken advantage of Rafe in high school.

I hadn't cracked the spine of a Barbara Botticelli romance since I realized who Barbara was, and that there was a reason every hero in every book she wrote reminded me of Rafe. The knowledge that every time the hero dropped his drawers, she'd imagined Rafe naked, had been enough to sour me on Barbara Botticelli ever after

Of course I'd also realized, after thinking about it, that her imagination couldn't compare to my reality. She'd based her heroes on Rafe at eighteen, drunk and in pain. I had him in my bed every night, and you can believe me, Elspeth's love scenes had nothing on mine. Her imagination had been woefully inadequate when it came to describing Rafe at thirty and thirty-one.

And anyway, she was dead. I should probably get over my aversion to the books and just be grateful that Rafe was still alive because she'd stood in front of him when someone was trying to kill him.

There was a new Botticelli book scheduled for release before Christmas. Her last. It had been in production when she died last fall, and Dix, as her executor, had been in touch with the publisher and given them the go-ahead to publish it. The money from the sale would come to David, so we'd all agreed that there was no sense in refusing. The manuscript was finished, and just needed editing. Might as well get it out there, for the fans who wanted it, and for David, who'd need money for college in a few years. By November, I might even want to read it.

But for now, I'd stick with the romance hero I had in my bed. A romance hero who was starting to wake up. In more ways than one. I heard his breathing change, and felt his body go from lax to aware. And then to alert. The part of him that was nestled against my derriere twitched.

I giggled. Waking up ready to take on the day, and anything

else in the vicinity, is a common male trait, but I never got tired of it.

"Feeling OK?" His voice was still gravelly from sleep, and his hand brushed over my stomach on its way north.

"Fine. I'm not nauseous anymore." That had ended with the first trimester. Now I just woke up hungry.

"Must be early," Rafe murmured as his hand continued exploring under the blankets.

"Why?"

"I don't smell any coffee. Or bacon. It's a bed and breakfast. There should be food."

There should. "It must be early." I stretched and pushed against him. He pushed back.

"That mean we have time for some exercise before we get outta bed?"

"I could be talked into it," I told him. My libido was up, too, with the pregnancy hormones. I could pretty much always be talked into it.

Then again, he hadn't had a problem talking me out of my clothes and into bed before I got pregnant, either.

"Ain't much of a talker, darlin'. How about I just show you?"

He proceeded to do just that. And it worked just as well.

As a result of this show and tell, it was at least another hour before we rolled out of bed and staggered into the shower. While Rafe rinsed off, I dug into the overnight bags, for something to wear, and to see whether there were any surprises inside. And whether Grimaldi had packed Rafe any underwear, or me any interesting toys.

I started with my own bag, which didn't contain anything out of the ordinary. I did have underwear, and a couple of light sundresses and pairs of sandals. She'd thrown in a hair brush, along with shampoo, dental floss, and toothpaste, but if I wanted any product for my hair—spray or mousse, gel or hot rollers—I was on my own. I foresaw a lot of ponytails in my future.

The only unusual item in my bag was a pair of men's swim trunks. My own bathing suit was there—a demure vintage-style polka-dotted one-piece with a halter top and ruffles at the hips— and along with it, a pair of navy board shorts with the tags still attached.

I hadn't seen them before, and for a moment I wondered whether Grimaldi had sent them so I could cover my rear. If so, they'd make me look worse than if I wore nothing over the bathing suit. Once I'd squashed myself and all those ruffles inside the shorts, I'd not only look broad in the beam, I'd look lumpy.

Then it occurred to me that maybe they were for Rafe, and had just ended up in the wrong bag. I pulled the zipper down on his to investigate.

It didn't yield anything of interest, either. Not at first glance. She *had* packed underwear, so he wouldn't have to spend our honeymoon commando. I wasn't sure whether to be happy or disappointed about that. Happy for him and disappointed for myself, I guess, although I rarely have a problem talking him out of his underwear, so it wasn't like it was a big deal either way.

No hair product for Rafe, either, and no hair brush. She had tossed in a couple pairs of T-shirts, a pair of jeans, and a halfway decent button-down shirt. In case we wanted to go somewhere nice for dinner one night, I guess.

But there was a swimsuit. And looking at it, I could understand why the navy trunks were in my bag and not his. She must have been anticipating the look on his face when he opened the bag and realized that if he wanted to go to the beach, he had a choice between jeans, tuxedo pants, and a pair of metallic gold Speedos.

Bikini style.

FOUR

"What the hell?"

While I'd been twirling the Speedos around on my finger and trying to picture how they would look wrapped around Rafe's hips, he had opened the door from the bathroom and caught me sitting there. He was still wet, with a white towel around his waist, beads of water running down his chest and his calves, and he had another towel in his hand and had been arrested mid-motion, in the middle of rubbing his hair dry. He was still holding the towel to the top of his head; he just wasn't moving his arm anymore.

Instead, his eyes were fastened on the scrap of metallic fabric spinning around my finger. "What's that?"

"Your swimsuit," I said, stopping the spinning and holding the Speedos up for his perusal.

He looked at them for a second, before moving his attention to me, and I think he must have been struck dumb, because when he opened his mouth, nothing came out.

"They were in your bag," I added. "I had no idea you owned a pair of metallic gold Speedos. I can't wait to see what they look like on."

The thought broke the spell. "I ain't wearing those." He sounded halfway between shocked and repulsed, but not amused at all.

"You can't go to the beach in tuxedo pants," I pointed out.

"Between tuxedo pants and whatever the hell that is, yes, I can." He tossed the towel on the bed, but didn't come any closer. Maybe he was afraid the Speedos would attack. He eyed them like he thought they might. "My junk won't fit in those."

Probably not, now that he mentioned it. Some men aren't built for Speedos, and Rafe is one of them.

"For me?" I batted my eyes at him.

He shook his head. "Not even for you, darlin'. Not in public."

"How about here? Now? Just so I can see?" Because while I could certainly understand why he wouldn't want to wear a pair of Speedos the size of a string bikini outside the room, I was dying to see what he looked like in them.

He sighed. "Fine. But if you try to take a picture of me, I'm breaking your phone." He reached out a hand.

I handed the scrap of gold fabric over. And lost my own ability to speak when he flicked the second towel open and it dropped to the floor.

Never mind the Speedos.

I couldn't get the words out. All I could do was sit and gape as he pulled the teeny-tiny piece of cloth up over his calves and thighs and butt and adjusted them.

In case you were in doubt, he has a beautiful body. Long legs, strong calves and thighs, narrow hips, and a muscular butt. Hard muscles under smooth, golden skin. He wouldn't look out of place modeling underwear on a billboard in Times Square.

But he's also well-endowed. The front of the Speedos bulged in a way that left absolutely nothing to the imagination. I'm not even sure the top edge of the fabric touched the skin of his stomach.

"No," I managed, my voice choked, "you can't go outside like that." I'd have to beat the women off with a stick. Or considering where we were, a piece of driftwood.

He arched a brow and turned to the mirror, hands on his hips. Silence reigned for a moment. I watched his glutei maximi—

plural—covered in metallic gold and concentrated on breathing.

In. Out. In...

"This your idea of a joke?" he asked eventually, with a glance at me in the mirror.

I shook my head. "Tamara Grimaldi packed the bags. I guess she put them there." And she was probably having a good laugh at our expense right now.

"For what it's worth," I added, now that I'd gotten my voice back, "you look incredible. But I'm not letting you out of this room in those."

"Not a problem. I wasn't going anywhere anyway." He hooked his thumbs in the sides of the Speedos and began peeling them down. My tongue got stuck to the roof of my mouth. When he was naked again, he turned to me, and grinned when he saw the look on my face. "How about we just stay up here the rest of the day?"

"How about we get something to eat and come back? I'm starving."

He shrugged. "Whatever you want. Guess we won't be spending much time on the beach, anyway."

"She got you a pair of board shorts, too." I pulled them out of my own bag and tossed them at him. "You'll probably like them better."

He did. And after he'd pulled them up and stuck his hand down the front to adjust the contents to his satisfaction, I had to admit he looked good enough to eat in those, too. A lot less X-rated than in the Speedos, but much safer for public consumption. After he'd pulled a plain white T-shirt down over his chest and stomach to hide all those delicious muscles, we headed out the door and down the stairs.

By then it was after nine, but there was still no smell of coffee or food in the air. When we got to the dining room, we saw why.

The rest of the guests were ranged around the big table in the middle of the room. I recognized them from the descriptions we'd gotten last night. Our blond friend was there, next to a dark-haired guy a few years older than Rafe, whose muscles were turning to fat. He looked petulant, with a sort of perpetual pout. On the other side of the table sat two women in their forties, and an older couple; surely the residents of number 3 and number 4. The folks from number 1 had styrofoam cups of coffee in front of them, but apart from that, there was nothing to eat or drink on the table or the sideboard, and no odor of food in the air.

All six of them looked up when we came through the door.

There was a moment of silence. As usual, most of the attention focused on Rafe. I'm used to that. Women look at him because he's gorgeous, and men look at him because... well, sometimes because he's gorgeous—like my colleague Tim, who's had a crush on Rafe for as long as he's known about him. But for most guys, it's more because he's big and strong and used to taking charge. It's an alpha-dog thing. *Is this guy bigger and stronger than me?*

More often than not, the answer is yes. A lot of men feel threatened by Rafe, and not always because he wants them to—although sometimes he does.

Now wasn't one of those times. He was off-duty, and had no need to throw his weight around. He was imposing enough just standing there, even in board shorts and a T-shirt, and I'm sure he knew it.

"I'm Rafe Collier," he said calmly. "This is my wife, Savannah. We got here late last night."

The blonde giggled. Her significant other glanced at her, but didn't say anything. It was one of the middle-aged women who spoke up. "I'm Gloria. This is Hildy." She glanced at her companion, who nodded to us.

"Groot Jenkins," the old guy said—at least I think he did. "My wife Vonnie."

Vonnie nodded.

The blonde flipped her hair over her shoulder. In the light, it looked more like cotton candy than ever: so bleached and treated and stripped of anything natural it looked like a tuft of hay glued to her head. "We met last night," she said. "I'm Nina," she pronounced it Nine-ah, "and this is Chip."

Chip nodded. The look he gave me was bordering on offensive; the one he gave Rafe assessing.

My stomach chose that moment to emit an unladylike rumble. I put a hand to it, and Hildy smiled. "You must be starving." She glanced at the butler door I assumed went to the kitchen.

"We thought breakfast was between eight and ten." Rafe glanced at Nina. "That's what you said, right?"

She nodded, with another hair flip. "I don't know where Frenetta is. Chip and I went out for breakfast. There's a coffee place down the street a couple of blocks. They have muffins and things."

I needed something more than a muffin, but I didn't bother saying so. A muffin wasn't likely to satisfy Rafe either, so he could say it for me.

"Has anyone seen her?"

Nobody had.

"Did she say anything about not being here?" I asked. "Like, 'you'll be responsible for feeding yourselves this morning?'"

"Not to me," Nina said, with a hair flip. It was starting to get on my nerves, and I'd only just met her. "But we didn't talk much."

"How long have you been here?"

She and Chip were from Atlanta, and they had driven down on Friday. Last night had been their second night at the Davenport Inn B and B.

Rafe glanced at Gloria, who told him, "She didn't say anything to me about not being here. You, Hildy?"

Hildy shook her head. "The last time I saw her was after dinner last night. She was in the kitchen when we came back from dinner. She was prepping some kind of pecan rolls for this morning."

"When was that?" Rafe wanted to know.

Hildy and Gloria looked at one another and decided it must have been around seven-thirty. "She was kneading dough in between sips of wine. We talked for a minute, and then Hildy and I went upstairs."

"Did anyone see her after that?" Rafe glanced around the table.

No one spoke up. Until Chip asked, in a disagreeable way, "You a cop or something?"

"Something," Rafe told him. "Anyone know where she sleeps?"

"Apartment above the garage," Nina said, with another toss of her head. "She said she needs to get away from here at night."

"Stay here."

He didn't wait to see if anyone obeyed, just headed for the back door. I decided to pretend that the order hadn't been directed at me, so after an apologetic smile at the assembled company, I hurried after him.

"Wait!"

By the time I caught up, he was already halfway across the parking lot, which did, in the light of day, turn out to be made up of crunched shells instead of gravel.

He glanced at me over his shoulder. "What part of 'stay here' didn't you understand?"

"We've been married less than twenty-four hours, and you're already giving me orders?"

I stuck my hand in his and hustled to keep up. His legs are considerably longer than mine, and he's in much better physical condition. Also, the shells were difficult to navigate on heels.

He didn't answer, and I added, "What are you afraid you'll find, that you don't want me to see?"

"You know what."

I did. Or I could guess. "What makes you think she's dead?"

"Nothing," Rafe said. "Except dead bodies seem to follow you around."

"They do not!" Most of the dead bodies I had encountered — or at least half of them — I could lay at Rafe's door. Not literally — in most cases he hadn't killed them — but they'd had more to do with him than with me.

"If it was earlier, I mighta thought she'd overslept, but it's after nine. And she didn't say nothing to nobody about going away. She was here last night, prepping for breakfast."

"She could be ill," I said.

"Maybe."

"Or perhaps she went to church. It's Sunday. Maybe she's coming back in an hour or two to make brunch."

He hesitated. "That ain't a bad idea, actually."

It wasn't. However — "We're here. We might as well knock and make sure nothing wrong."

We had reached the bottom of the staircase leading up to the second floor above the garage. There was only room for one person to ascend at a time, and Rafe dropped my hand. "If you don't wanna wait down here, at least let me go up first."

"No problem."

I waited for him to start up, and then I followed.

At the top of the stairs, he knocked on the door.

There was no answer, and I don't think either of us expected one.

"Try the knob," I said.

He wrapped the bottom of his T-shirt around his hand before doing so.

The door opened with a squeak of hinges. Nothing that should have given anyone a fright, not in the bright, hot sunlight of the Florida morning. Nonetheless, I felt a cold trickle down my spine. Or maybe it was just the blast of frigid air that flooded out through the open door. Frenetta must keep her AC at morgue setting.

"Hello? Miz... um..."

"Wallin," I whispered.

He glanced at me before raising his voice again. "Miz Wallin? Anyone home?"

No one answered.

I added my voice to his, just in case Frenetta was worried about an unknown man on her doorstop. "Miss Wallin? This is Savannah Martin. Um... Collier."

Rafe shot me an amused look. I ignored it, just kept talking to the silent apartment. "We arrived last night. Are you home?"

But she didn't answer my call, either.

"Should we go in?" I asked Rafe.

He shrugged. "Might as well. The door's open. And I ain't carrying, so it's misdemeanor trespass, at best."

"Isn't there a rule that says if you think someone's in imminent danger, you can break in?"

Rafe nodded. "She ain't in danger. She's gone. One way or the other." He nudged the door open wider and raised his voice again as he stepped across the threshold. "Miz Wallin? We're coming inside. Can you hear me?"

There was no answer, only the sound of his footsteps as he moved across the tile floors. I followed, looking left and right.

It wasn't a big space. It was just the top floor of a garage, after all. One medium-sized room served as a combination living room and dining room, with an apartment-sized kitchen tucked into the corner. Small fridge, four-burner stove, on-the-counter microwave. An open door next to the kitchen led to a small washroom: I could see the edge of a sink and most of the toilet. There was probably a shower beyond the wall.

Another door just beyond it was closed, and that's where Rafe was headed. I watched as he applied his knuckles to the wood. "Miz Wallin? Are you there?"

This time he didn't bother to wait for an answer. He just stuck his hand into his T-shirt once more, and twisted the knob.

Like the front door, this door—to the bedroom, I assumed— opened without a problem. Frenetta was either very trusting, or someone else had left all the doors open.

There was no squeak this time. And no chill creeping down my spine.

"Stay here," Rafe told me as he crossed the threshold into the bedroom.

This time I listened. The bedroom was tiny. I could see from where I was standing that Frenetta was in bed, curled up on her side under a blue blanket, and that she wasn't breathing. I had no need to go any closer. Rafe did, and although I'm sure he could see, just as well as I could, that there was no movement in the body under the blanket, he put two fingers against Frenetta's throat. After a few seconds, he shook his head.

"Died in her sleep?" My voice was soft.

Rafe shrugged and took a step back, stuffing both hands in the pockets of his shorts. "No idea."

I moved a stop closer and looked up at him. "They'll have to do an autopsy, I guess."

He nodded.

"Any sign of what killed her?"

"If I was a coroner," Rafe said, "I might could tell you that. But so far, I've made more corpses than I've treated."

"That's a horrible thing to say! You haven't killed that many people."

"More than you," Rafe said, which was true. Then again, my record wasn't hard to beat. I'd killed one person, and a week later, was still struggling with that fact. It had been him or me, I knew that. I'd been trying to defend myself, as well as Mother and David, but I hadn't been trying to kill him.

But I digress. Rafe had killed two people that I knew of, because I'd been there, and he had come close a third time. The guy had survived, though, and was serving twenty-five to life in a Georgia prison. I thought there might have been someone in the line of duty at some point as well, but I'd never asked. There were a lot of things Rafe had done before I met him again, that I figured I'd just as soon not know about.

Mostly because I figured his past included rather a lot of women.

"Her lips are blue. That means something, right?"

"Usually means hypothermia." He glanced around. "It's cold in here, but I don't think it's that cold."

It wasn't. Frenetta had kept her apartment at a chilly sixty-nine degrees, but that's not cold enough to freeze anyone to death.

"What else?"

"Some kinds of poisoning," Rafe said. "Alcohol, I think."

"Alcohol poisoning?"

He nodded.

"There's a wine glass on the side table."

There was, with a smear of red in the bottom. The way the light hit it, made it look like blood, but I knew it was just residue from red wine. There was no blood anywhere in the bedroom, and no sign of anything untoward. Frenetta was curled up on her side like she were asleep—to the degree that the dead ever look like they sleep—with her eyes closed and the blanket pulled up to her chin. If anything criminal had happened here, and she hadn't just died peacefully in her sleep, it had happened very quietly, without leaving any hint that it had happened at all.

Rafe sighed. "I guess we've seen enough."

He reached for his pocket, and I assume his phone, and that's when a voice said, "Hold it right there." It cracked on the last syllable, either from excitement or fear, and its owner had to clear his throat before he added, "Hands in the air and turn around slowly."

FIVE

"Is this really necessary?" I asked three minutes later.

We were downstairs in the parking lot, and the young sheriff's deputy—who was probably wishing with all his might that he was off-duty today—had told Rafe to assume the position against the hood of the Volvo.

He had patted me down already—very gently and politely, probably because Rafe had been staring at him with that patented *'would you like to die now, or later?'* look on his face the whole time. Now it was his turn, and although Rafe was obeying without much of a fuss, the young cop looked reluctant to venture any closer.

I couldn't blame him. He looked eighteen, although he was probably a few years older, if he was a full-fledged sheriff's deputy, and he was no taller than me. Since he was of Asian ancestry, that wasn't surprising, but standing next to Rafe's muscular six-foot-three, he looked like a child. My husband could break him like a twig.

And Rafe was unhappy. "Listen, kid," he said, legs apart and hands braced on the hood of the car, so the muscles in his upper arms stretched the sleeves of the T-shirt, "I ain't carrying. We're on our honeymoon. I left my gun at home."

This assurance didn't seem to make the young man any happier.

"He's a TBI agent," I explained. "The Tennessee Bureau of

Investigations. He's allowed to carry a gun. And if you ask nicely, I'm sure he'll show you his badge."

Rafe glanced at me over his shoulder. "That's at home too, darlin'. I didn't figure I'd need my gun and badge this weekend. I know your mama don't like me much, but I didn't think things'd go far enough that I'd need to shoot nobody."

"He's a TBI agent," I told Deputy Chang. "You can trust me."

Rafe rolled his eyes and turned back to the car. "Been a while since I had to deal with this shit. I forgot how much I don't like it."

I hadn't particularly liked it, either, despite the deputy's polite manner. There's just something inherently demeaning about being patted down. And for Rafe, who had been on the receiving end of that kind of treatment more than anyone should be, I'm sure it was doubly annoying. After ten years of having everyone in the world believing he was a criminal, he was finally in a place where things were working well. He had a good job, everyone knew he was an upstanding citizen, even my mother had grudgingly admitted that I could do worse. He had a new wife and a baby on the way... and this kind of thing kept happening to him.

"C'mon, kid," he growled. "I ain't wearing nothing but a T-shirt and a pair of shorts. There's nowhere to hide a weapon in this getup. Just do it. I don't wanna spend the whole day standing here."

Chang swallowed, but approached. Although he kept his hand on the butt of his gun. In case Rafe made a sudden move, I guess. I could have told him—although I didn't—that if Rafe made a move, that gun wouldn't have a chance to clear the holster. Hopefully Rafe wasn't thinking of doing anything that stupid.

He didn't. Just stood there, visibly simmering, while Chang made sure that he wasn't hiding anything lethal in his board shorts.

Then Chang stepped back to a safe distance. "OK. You can turn around."

Rafe turned around. I wandered over to him, now that we both were cleared, and he put an arm around me. "What's going on?" he asked Chang.

"We got a call," Chang said. "About a B&E in progress at this address."

Rafe's lips tightened. "Who called it in?"

"Don't know," Chang said. When Rafe didn't bother to look like he believed him, Chang added, "I didn't talk to them. The dispatcher took the call and told me to go check it out. I got here in time to see the two of you go inside Miz Wallin's place."

"We're guests at the inn," I explained, although we'd already been over this upstairs in Frenetta's apartment, before Chang had hustled us down the stairs and into the parking lot. "She didn't show up for breakfast this morning. We thought we'd check on her."

"So you went up to her apartment and broke in."

"The door was open," Rafe said. "Misdemeanor trespass. I ain't carrying."

This time it was Chang's lips that tightened. I deduced that Rafe knew more than Chang liked about the legalities of the situation.

"Besides," I added, "we weren't planning to commit a crime. We were concerned."

"Because Miz Wallin didn't show up for breakfast."

"Because Ms. Wallin didn't show up to cook and serve breakfast. She runs a B and B, Deputy. Cooking and serving breakfast is part of the job."

Chang sighed. "Tell me what happened."

I told him what had happened. Our arrival yesterday, and the fact that Frenetta hadn't been here to greet us. "Although it was pretty late. Nina wasn't happy about having to come downstairs to open the door for us." At least not until she'd seen Rafe.

"Nina?"

"One of the other guests. There are four guest rooms upstairs. We're in number 2. Nina and Chip are in 1, Hildy and Gloria are in 3, and Groot and Vonnie are in 4."

Chang looked overwhelmed.

"Write it down," Rafe growled, and Chang gave him a resentful look.

"Be nice," I told him. Rafe, not Chang. Chang and I weren't on those terms. Not yet. "He's just doing his job. And he's probably not used to dealing with dead bodies. Pretend he's one of your boys. You don't yell at them, do you?"

"Sure I do." But he made a visible effort to calm down. "Listen, kid..."

"And don't call him that. I don't think he likes it."

Rafe gave me a look that said he didn't like being told what to do, either, but he followed the advice. "Listen, Deputy," he said, with a sideways glance at me to make sure I appreciated how restrained he was, "my wife and I got here late last night. We never even met Miz Wallin. All we did was check and see if she was all right, since everybody else was just sitting around waiting for something to happen."

"He's used to taking charge," I told Chang, and earned myself another look from Rafe. "Well, you are. And anyway, we just wanted to make sure she was all right. Nobody answered when we knocked, but the door was open, so we went in. And we found her in bed. Dead."

"How did you know she was dead? Did you touch her?"

"I checked for a pulse," Rafe said. "The body's cold, and rigor mortis has set in."

For someone who isn't used to dealing with dead bodies, he sure sounded official.

"Of course the body's cold," I said. "It's like a meat locker up there."

And maybe that wasn't the best analogy, because they both

turned to stare at me.

"Sorry," I said. "I'll just stand here and be quiet, shall I?"

"Thanks, darlin'," Rafe answered, and turned back to Chang. "There was no sign of anything suspicious, other than the open door. And she coulda forgotten to lock it. Or maybe this is the kind of town where people don't bother to lock their doors at night."

"The B and B door was locked," I reminded him.

He glanced at me, but didn't answer. "I don't know nothing about this woman. For all I know, she coulda been in the habit of leaving her door open. She coulda been expecting someone. She coulda been planning to go out, and forgot."

Chang nodded. "You arrived last night? How long are you staying?"

We told him, and answered a couple more questions—the lights had been out in the parking lot last night; no, we hadn't noticed any lights on in the apartment, either; no, we hadn't seen anyone but Nina—and then Chang said we could go. "But don't leave town."

"I know the drill, Deputy," Rafe said. "We ain't going nowhere for the next couple days. Like I said, we're on our honeymoon. Is it OK if we go down to the beach?"

"You can go anywhere in town," Chang said expansively, as if that included more than just a square half mile, "just don't leave."

We said we wouldn't, and walked away. Chang went into the B and B, I assume to talk to the other guests and give them the news that Frenetta was no longer among the living.

"This is awkward."

Rafe glanced down at me. "Not sure that's the word I woulda used."

"I meant that our hostess is dead. How can we stay on in a house where the hostess is dead? It seems like very bad manners."

"I don't think Chang's gonna let us leave," Rafe said.

"But we never even met Frenetta. Why would we want to kill her?"

"Why would anybody?" He didn't wait for me to answer, just added, "What do you mean, kill? You don't know that she didn't die peacefully in her sleep."

No, I didn't. I guess I'd just gotten used to the corpses I encountered getting that way as a result of unnatural circumstances. But he was right. There'd been no evidence of foul play—other than that unlocked door, and Frenetta could have forgotten to lock it. And the blue lips... well, I'm sure there are lots of reasons why someone's lips might turn blue, and not all of them unnatural.

"She didn't look very old, though. Too young to die in her sleep for no reason."

Best guess, I'd put Frenetta's age at somewhere between sixty and sixty-five. And while people die at that age, it's usually because something's wrong with them.

"You dunno that something wasn't wrong with her," Rafe said, and stopped as we came out between the last two houses and stood opposite from the beach. "There it is."

There it was. And we could see it so much better than last night. The sand was almost white, sugary, and the ocean a light turquoise or teal, bluer than the sky, with tiny, froth-capped waves.

"It's gorgeous."

Rafe nodded. When he turned to me, his eyes were lit up like a kid's. "Let's go."

"You go." I was wearing a sundress. I wasn't about to throw myself into the waves.

"You sure?"

I nodded. Rafe whipped the T-shirt over his head and tossed it to me with a grin, and started running, straight for the water.

I watched him for a few seconds, and then wandered off to find shade. Being burnt to a crisp is unladylike, and tanning gives you wrinkles. So I found an empty umbrella, pushed a couple of quarters into the slot in the stem to get it to open, and settled in a lounge chair to watch Rafe play in the waves.

He was like a little kid seeing the ocean for the first time. If he'd had a bucket and spade, I think he would have built a sand castle.

He seemed blissfully unconcerned with the cross-stitch of healing scars across his chest and abdomen, and with the two-inch stab wound going straight through his lower arm, still pink and puffy. The bandage had come off just in time for the wedding. They weren't his first scars, by any means, so I guess he just regarded them as par for the course, but I felt a little shiver go down my spine every time I looked at him. For a horrible eighteen hours or so, I hadn't been sure I'd ever see him again. The fact that he had acquired another twenty or thirty scars during that time, didn't bother me in the least. The fact that the person who gave them to him—the person whose name was carved into his skin along with that crazy-quilt pattern—could have, and had, every intention of killing him when he was finished amusing himself, upset me a lot more.

Rafe seemed to have shaken it off. He didn't talk about the experience, and didn't seem to dwell on it. And if the scars bothered him, he didn't show it. He did get a few sideways glances, though. Some of them, I'm sure, just because he's exceptionally gorgeous half-dressed, but I caught a few double-takes and shocked expressions thrown his way, as well. If those bothered him, he didn't let that show, either.

I let him play for as long as I could stand it, and the next time he came back to the umbrella, I told him, "I'm starving. Any chance we could go get some early lunch somewhere?"

"Christ." He looked immediately chastised. "Course, darlin'. You shoulda said something sooner."

"I didn't really notice until now," I fibbed. He gave me a jaundiced look, and I added, "Fine. You were having so much fun

I didn't want you to have to stop. But now I really do need to eat something. I think the baby's starting to gnaw on my stomach lining."

"Let's hope not." He held out his hand for his T-shirt, and I handed it over and watched as he pulled it down over muscles, scars, and everything else. "What're you hungry for?"

It took me a second to drag my gaze up to meet his, and he chuckled. "If you want some of that, you gotta keep your strength up. Let's get you fed first." He reached out a hand to haul me to my feet.

"I don't really care what I eat," I told him as I put my hand in his. "It depends on what's available."

"Then let's take a walk and see." He kept my hand in his as we wandered off down the beach, eying the store fronts on the other side of the street, and the food carts parked on the beach walk.

It didn't take long to find something acceptable, probably because I was so hungry that almost anything would have sounded good to me. Rafe likes pizza, so we ended up in a pizza parlor where he grabbed a couple of slices, and I ordered a salad. The baby had given me a tendency toward heartburn, so I was trying to avoid both spicy—tomato sauce—and greasy—melted cheese—foods for the time being.

It was while we were sitting there, chomping on pizza and lettuce leaves, that Deputy Chang came back into our lives. The bell above the door rang. Rafe glanced up, and I could see his expression become resigned. When I turned to look over my shoulder, I saw Chang bearing down on us. "Mr. Collier? I'm going to have to ask you to accompany me to the sheriff's office."

"Found out about my record, did you?"

Chang didn't answer, and Rafe added, "Just gimme a minute to finish lunch with my wife, Deputy. I'll be right with you."

Chang nodded and went to take up position next to the door. I guess he wanted to make sure that Rafe wouldn't have a chance to make a break for it.

"I thought your record was expunged," I told him as soon as Chang was out of range.

He shook his head, conveying the last few bites of pepperoni pizza to his mouth. "Nothing I did undercover stuck. But I earned that stretch in Riverbend all on my own."

Five years for aggravated assault and felony battery with the intent to cause harm. Two years served before the TBI talked him into going undercover for them. He was barely eighteen when it happened, and just twenty when they let him out.

It was a lifetime ago. He was a different person now. It was a damn shame that after everything he'd done, it was still following him around, causing trouble.

"Do I need to call Dix and get a recommendation for a lawyer?" I wanted to know.

He shook his head. "I ain't worried yet. Unless they're stupid, they're gonna figure out that I didn't have nothing to do with it. We've never been here before, and didn't know the lady."

I nodded. "Do you want me to come with you?"

He shook his head again. "No sense in us both sitting at the sheriff's office. Just go back to the B and B and take a nap. The sun prob'ly made you sleepy."

It had, especially coupled with the food. And of course the baby. I was tired all the time nowadays.

"Are you sure?"

"I'm positive," Rafe said and pushed his chair back. "I'll see you in a couple hours."

He took the time to bend and drop a kiss on my lips, and then he sauntered toward the door, where Chang was still waiting. As they passed through and out into the blinding sunshine, it was hard to say who looked more relaxed, the cop or the ex-con.

I cleaned off the table and headed out, while people stared and whispered. I ignored it, something I've gotten better at since taking up with Rafe. There was a time when the idea of being the center of attention, of having people talk about me, was the worst thing imaginable.

A lady doesn't draw attention to herself, darling.

I could almost hear my mother's voice.

But that was all behind me now. Let'em stare. Who cared what they thought, about him, me, or any of it? After tomorrow, we'd never see any of them again anyway.

By the time I got outside to the sidewalk, Chang's patrol car was gone, and so, of course, was Rafe. I trudged back to the B and B, but before I made it upstairs and to bed, I was waylaid by Gloria and Hildy, who were sitting on the front porch sipping lemonade.

"There you are!" Gloria said when she saw me.

It seemed impolite to simply nod and walk past, so I made myself stop. "Hello."

"We wondered where you'd got to!"

"We went to the beach," I said. "And then to lunch."

"And where's your handsome husband?"

She peered down the street, maybe thinking he had let me walk back to the B and B on my own, and was coming.

"Deputy Chang came and picked him up," I said.

That seemed to be the opening they'd been looking for, because they both leaned forward. "He said Frenetta's dead," Hildy said, her voice hushed.

I nodded.

"What happened?"

"I have no idea. She was in bed. I guess maybe she just... died."

They exchanged a look. "She wasn't very old," Gloria said.

Hildy shook her head. "Old enough that she'd want to retire, but not old enough to die."

"Maybe she was ill?" I suggested.

They exchanged another look. "I didn't notice anything like

that," Gloria said. Hildy shook her head.

I decided that since I was here, I might as well get some information. It would keep my mind occupied, and off Rafe, in the process of being grilled by Deputy Chang at the sheriff's office.

I was hopeful that Chang and his boss would see that Rafe wasn't involved in Frenetta's death, in spite of that arrest record. But the possibility that they wouldn't was playing with my mind, so I could use a distraction. This one would work.

I pulled an unoccupied wicker chair closer to the porch swing where Gloria and Hildy sat, and sank down in it. "You said you'd been here a while, right?"

They nodded in unison. It was weird to see them so in sync, since they looked totally different. Gloria was handsome rather than pretty, with cropped hair, broad shoulders under a striped shirt, and muscular legs in khaki shorts. Hildy, on the other hand, was all girl, with a messy topknot of frizzy gray-streaked brown hair, and a frumpy summer dress with little flowers.

"We got here late last night," I continued, "and I think Frenetta may already have been dead. At least she didn't come down to greet us, and there were no lights on in her apartment."

They both nodded.

"So we never actually met her. And since it was my sister who made the reservation, I never even spoke to her on the phone." Although maybe I should give Catherine a call and get her impression of the deceased. Or at least let her know what was going on.

Thanks, sis. Just what we needed. A busman's honeymoon.

Like we didn't have enough crime in our regular lives.

"This is our third time here," Gloria said. Hildy made a sort of aborted movement, and Gloria glanced at her, but didn't stop speaking. "We came down from Massachusetts last summer and fell in love with the place. Then we came back over Christmas, and now we're back again."

"So you must have gotten to know Frenetta pretty well. Any idea who might have wanted to do away with her?"

There was a pause. "What makes you think someone did away with her?" Gloria asked.

"Was she...?" Hildy paused delicately.

I shook my head. "It looked like she'd gone to sleep and never woken up." Aside from the blue lips. "But if the police are interviewing suspects, they must think she didn't die a natural death."

Or at least they were open to the possibility.

"And your husband's a *suspect*?" Hildy asked. "How awful for you!"

I shrugged. "I'm used to it." Not that it ever got any easier, but for a while, every time Rafe showed up in Sweetwater, Sheriff Satterfield tried to pin something on him. By now, I wasn't even surprised when someone prejudged him based on the way he looked and the fact that he had a prison record. "So any ideas about who might have wanted Frenetta dead? Or why?"

They exchanged a glance. "She could be trying," Gloria said. "Indecisive. She'd make up her mind, and then change it five minutes later. You never really knew where you stood. Although I don't know that that's enough for someone to kill her..."

"Do you know if she had any differences with anyone? Any arguments?"

They looked at one another. "Go ahead and tell her," Hildy said.

"Tell me what?"

Gloria lowered her voice. "Yesterday morning, when we came down to breakfast, she and Nina were in the butler's pantry. Talking."

"Arguing," Hildy said.

"Did you hear what they were arguing about?"

"Chip," Gloria said.

"Chip?"

They both nodded.

"Why?"

"We don't know," Gloria said. "But we very distinctly heard his name." She lowered her voice, after a quick look around to make sure no one was listening. "Nina threatened Frenetta."

"Threatened her? Really?"

Gloria nodded. "I heard her say, 'You'd better do right by Chip, or else.'"

"Or else, what?"

"She didn't say," Gloria said. "But I could tell it wouldn't be good."

Hildy nodded.

"Did you tell the police?"

They both shook their heads. "They didn't ask."

"Did she see you? Nina?"

They exchanged a glance. "When she came out of the butler's pantry. Why?"

"Because if she killed Frenetta, and she knows you overheard her threaten Frenetta, she might decide to get rid of you, too."

Hildy gulped, and Gloria paled.

I got to my feet. "If I were you, I'd tell the police." Hopefully that'd be enough to remove some of the suspicion from Rafe. "As soon as possible. Better safe than sorry."

I left them sitting there, looking a lot less relaxed than when I'd arrived.

SIX

Rafe didn't come back for hours.

I had finally fallen asleep, after spending what felt like an eternity fretting and wondering whether he'd come back at all, or whether I'd get a phone call telling me I had to arrange for bail. But then I woke up an hour later to the feeling of something heavy descending on the side of the bed, and a pair of lips fitting themselves over mine.

It's a nice way to wake up. I stretched luxuriously, at the same time as I reached up and wrapped my arms around his neck, all of it without opening my eyes. I knew it was him, from the scent and the taste and the feel of him, achingly familiar by now.

One thing led to another, and it was thirty minutes later that I finally got around to asking, "How did it go at the sheriff's office?"

By now, Rafe was naked and next to me on the bed, flopped on his back catching his breath. It took him a moment to answer. "I'm here."

"I noticed. So at least they didn't arrest you. Is that what you're saying?"

He shrugged. Not an easy thing to do, lying down.

"Was there a chance they would?"

"Seemed like it for a bit."

"That's not good," I said.

He shook his head. "I'm sick of this prison record coming

back to bite my ass. Wish I woulda never touched Billy Scruggs."

I wished he hadn't, too. If anything should have the right to bite his posterior, it should be me. And the conviction would probably dog him for the rest of his life. Never mind that it was one single stupid mistake made by an eighteen-year-old kid whose mother had been beaten black and blue by her boyfriend, and that he had spent the past ten years risking his life every day to make up for it. As long as it was on his record, people wouldn't allow him to forget.

"Maybe I shouldn't forget," he told me when I said so. "I almost killed the bastard."

"And he killed your mother."

He had no answer for that. Just kept looking at the ceiling. I turned over on my stomach—harder to do these days; a little bit like trying to get comfortable balanced on top of a beach ball—and leaned on his chest. "I love you."

He glanced at me. "I love you, too."

"I'm glad they didn't keep you."

He nodded. "Me, too."

"Did it really look like they might?"

"It might could," Rafe said. "Whoever finds the body is always a suspect. Add in two years for assault and battery, and I'm sure they were prepping the handcuffs."

"So what happened?"

"We talked," Rafe said. "I had'em call Wendell, but since it's the weekend, ain't like there's anybody at the TBI who could verify that I work for them. And Wendell could be anybody."

"We could ask Grimaldi to go to the house and find your ID and scan it here. She's able to get in. She packed our bags."

"I'm sure Tammy's still in Sweetwater," Rafe said. "And I ain't calling her to save my butt. Anyway, they let me go."

"No evidence?"

"That," Rafe said. "And they got a phone call."

"What kind of phone call?"

"From somebody saying that Nina Hickman had been arguing with Frenetta yesterday morning."

Looked like Hildy and Gloria had come through. I smiled.

Rafe eyed me. "You know something about that?"

"I might. Hildy and Gloria were sitting on the porch when I came back here after lunch. I stopped to talk to them." I told him what they had told me. "I advised them to call the cops."

"Thanks."

"I didn't do it just for you," I told him. "If Nina killed Frenetta, she wouldn't be above killing Gloria and Hildy, too." Or any of the rest of us.

"Big step from arguing with somebody to killing them."

Sure. But— "I just wanted to give the cops another suspect to concentrate on. Someone actually viable. It's stupid for them to focus on you. We weren't even here until ten o'clock last night. We never met Frenetta. They need to look at people with a reason to want her dead."

Rafe nodded.

"And as long as they were wasting time on you, they weren't looking at anyone else."

Rafe shook his head.

"Out of curiosity, did they determine that it was murder? That she didn't just die in her sleep?"

"They think she was asphyxiated," Rafe said. "Maybe with something in the wine first, to knock her out and make her sleep. And then someone walked right in and smothered her."

I suppressed a shudder. I'd just been in here, sleeping, dead to the world, until he walked in. Someone—someone else—could have come in and asphyxiated me, as well. "That's horrible. But at least she didn't know it was happening."

"Not sure that makes it any better," Rafe said, and I guess that was true. He'd certainly want a chance to fight back when it was his turn. Me, I thought I might just want to sleep through it.

But hopefully it would be a lot of years before either of us had to worry about that.

Fat chance, my subconscious told me. I ignored it. Or tried to.

"Do you think Nina killed Frenetta?"

"Dunno," Rafe said. "They coulda been arguing about the mattress. Or the towels. Or something else that don't mean nothing."

Of course they could have. Maybe the mattress had aggravated Chip's lumbago, and Nina wanted a discount on the room rate to make up for it.

Or they could have argued about something important. But there was no way to know, and no way to find out. If we asked, Nina probably wouldn't tell us. Especially if she really had killed Frenetta.

"I'm hungry," I said.

"We just had lunch," Rafe answered.

"We had lunch five hours ago. You've just been so busy you haven't noticed. And I just worked out hard."

"Then let's go get you food." He rolled over to the edge of the bed and sat up. I watched for a second—there were no scars on his back; just beautiful smooth skin over hard muscles, and two dimples above his butt—and then I rolled on my side, too, and sat up.

Five minutes later we were on our way down the stairs to the foyer.

"You know," I told Rafe, "I feel really weird about being here. It's like we're just carrying right on with our honeymoon, but our hostess is dead."

He glanced at me, one hand under my elbow to make sure I didn't slip on the steps. "The sheriff told me not to leave, darlin'. And we don't have nowhere else to go in a town this size."

No. Unlike many of the Gulf Coast communities, Davenport hadn't succumbed to the highrise-condo-building-on-the-beach craze. There might be another motel or B and B somewhere in town, but I hadn't noticed one. If we had to stay in Davenport, we might as well stay where we were. However— "As soon as we can, I'd like to go home. I don't care if Catherine paid for our stay up front. Frenetta's dead. I would prefer not to stay here any longer than we have to."

He shrugged, and let go of my arm as we hit the downstairs foyer. "Works for me."

"I'd rather just go home and have my way with you in the privacy of our own house. Where nobody's knocking the bed against the wall all night." Except the two of us.

His lips quirked. "Maybe they'll be too overcome by guilt to do that tonight."

"We weren't," I said.

"We didn't kill her, darlin'."

Well, no. But— "They may not have, either. You don't kill somebody over towels or cinnamon rolls."

"Some people kill other people over fifty cents," Rafe said, as we passed through the foyer.

"Well, if they didn't, who d'you think did?"

He shrugged.

"It had to be someone with a motive. Maybe one of the townspeople. They'd know her better than a guest. The better you know someone, the more likely you'll be to want to kill them, right?"

"Not sure I like the sound of that, darlin'," Rafe told me, as he closed the door behind him.

I stuck my hand through his arm and rubbed my cheek on his shoulder as we headed down the stairs. "I'm sure I'll end up wanting to kill you at some point. Although I haven't yet. From where I'm standing, you're pretty much perfect."

"Awww."

"I love you," I said.

"I love you, too. And I promise I won't ever kill you."

"I didn't think you would. Like I said, you're perfect."

"Not hardly," Rafe said, as we approached the white picket

fence. "But hold that thought."

He opened the gate and waited for me to pass through before closing it behind me. Then he offered his arm again, with a little bow. "Ma'am."

"Don't mind if I do," I said, hooking on. "So what kind of food are you in the mood for?"

"We're by the ocean. We should probably look for seafood."

"I suppose." I wrinkled my nose. I'm not terribly fond of seafood, to be honest. It smells fishy, and sometimes it has an unpleasantly rubbery consistency, too.

"Burger?" Rafe said. "I'm sure there's a McDonald's around. There are McDonald's everywhere."

"No, thank you." To the burger and to McDonald's. Neither sounded appetizing in my current condition, either.

"Pizza parlor for another salad?"

It was nice of him to offer. However—"If you want seafood, we'll get you seafood. I'm sure I can find something to eat."

"There's a place a couple blocks down I heard good things about."

"That's fine. Who told you good things about it?"

"The sheriff," Rafe said.

I arched my brows. "You and the sheriff got to a point where you were friendly enough to exchange restaurant recommendations?"

"The recommendations only went one way. Sheriff Engebretsen wants people to have a good time in town. And spend money."

"Isn't that the mayor?"

"They all do," Rafe said and pointed. "There it is."

I followed the direction of his finger. "Where?"

"There. On the beach."

I looked again, but all I saw was a driftwood shack on stilts, up above the sand, with a neon sign in the window blinking on and off.

Actually, two neon signs. One said *OPEN*, and didn't blink. The blinking one said *Corona*, with an image of a parrot.

"That's the restaurant the sheriff recommended?"

It looked like a low-end biker bar. In fact, there was a handful of bikes parked outside, that looked very much like the one parked in our driveway at home. Big, beefy Harley-Davidsons with lots of chrome and fancy handlebars.

The first time I'd seen Rafe astride the beast, in Mrs. Jenkins's driveway the morning Brenda Puckett died, I'd been attracted and appalled in about equal measure. Big, noisy, masculine, and *so* uncouth.

Needless to say, he'd changed my mind later.

"The shrimp po'boys are supposed to be great."

Of course.

"And they have alligator tail. Have you ever had gator tail?"

I hadn't. "I bet it tastes just like chicken." That's what they say about anything out of the ordinary. Frog legs? Tastes just like chicken. Rattlesnake? Tastes just like chicken. Pigeon? Tastes just like chicken. Iguana? You got it. Tastes like chicken.

Rafe grinned. "Now that you mention it."

"If you want to have alligator tail, I won't stop you. And I'd be willing to try a shrimp po'boy." Which—for those of you born north of the Mason-Dixon line—is a sandwich. A Louisiana hoagie.

"That's all right," Rafe told me, as we left the road and wandered into the parking lot of the Sandbar. "I'm sure we can find something that isn't seafood. If they have shrimp po'boys, they might have roast beef ones, too."

"A roast beef sandwich would be OK."

"Then let's see what we've got," Rafe said, and opened the door.

The interior of the Sandbar looked about like I had expected. Not like I had wanted—it was my honeymoon, and I had envisioned eating gourmet seafood in a dining room with white tablecloths and stemware—but like I figured it would. A long, low, dark room with exposed wood beams in the ceiling, a rustic, sandy floor, no AC, and rough wooden tables with benches around them. The drinks came in cans, bottles, and red plastic cups, and the food arrived on paper plates or in little plastic baskets lined with fake newsprint. A nod to the old way of serving fish and chips, I guess.

But the Sandbar was hopping. Burly bikers in wife-beater shirts and suspenders rubbed elbows with sunburned kids and their exhausted parents. One TV was tuned to NASCAR, while the other showed an episode of SpongeBob SquarePants. It was hot and airless—the fans didn't do near enough to move the air through the open windows onto the deck overlooking the beach and ocean—but nobody seemed to care. People were laughing and chattering and obviously having a ball.

Rafe grinned. It was his kind of place. It wasn't mine, although I'm getting better about slumming. Mother would have had a conniption, but all I said was, "Can we see if there are any empty seats outside?"

"Sure." Rafe took my hand and pulled me after him through the room and out on the other side. It was much easier to breathe out on the deck, and a bit less crowded.

And there was Nina and Chip, over at a table in the corner, each with a liter glass of beer in front of them.

"Look." I nodded in that direction. "Let's go join them."

"They might not wanna be joined, darlin'." But he went. "Evening."

They both looked up. Chip grumbled something and Nina smiled. Widely. "Well, hello, there."

I resisted the temptation to roll my eyes. "Mind if we join you? This place is pretty busy."

There was a pause, while they tried to think of a way to say no without sounding rude. They couldn't, so they ended up allowing it. Rudely. Chip muttered under his breath as he moved over to make room for me, while Nina scooted aside just far enough to let Rafe sit down next to her. The better to press her naked thigh up against his, I assume.

It's a good thing I'm not the jealous type.

He gave her a cheerful grin as he sat down. I gave Chip a tight smile. He grumbled and took a swig of beer.

"Fancy meeting you here," Nina said brightly. She was dressed in the same—or a similar—white tank top as this morning, and her skin was the color of a walnut. By the time she reached forty, she'd be as leathery as a mummy.

"I didn't expect to run into you here," I told Chip, since Nina was busy exerting her charms on Rafe.

He slanted a grumpy glance at me. "Why?"

"We heard you had to go to the sheriff's office to talk about Frenetta's murder."

It could have been my imagination—it was dark out here—but I thought he turned a shade paler. "Murder?"

"They wouldn't interview suspects in a natural death," I said, and smiled at the waitress who stopped next to the table. "I'd like a glass of ginger ale, please."

Chip sniffed.

"And a menu."

The girl nodded and turned to Rafe, who said, "Draft."

The waitress sauntered off, and I turned back to Chip. "When they spoke to you this afternoon, didn't you get the impression that they were investigating a suspicious death?"

He didn't answer, just gave me a sullen look. It was Nina who spoke, from across the table. "Somebody told them that I'd been arguing with Frenetta yesterday morning. Like it was any of their business." She flipped her hair.

"I guess they figured, since she ended up dead, they'd make it their business."

It was Nina's turn to give me a look. "Not the cops. I

understand that they have to figure out who killed her. We want them to figure out who killed her." She glanced at Chip and then back to me. "I was talking about those two biddies."

"Gloria and Hildy?"

She nodded. "I should have known they overheard me. I didn't hear them coming down the stairs, but then they were there in the dining room." She shook her head. "I don't understand why people just can't mind their own business."

Chip snorted. "Just trying to make themselves look less bad."

"What do you mean?"

For a second I wasn't sure he'd answer—I don't think he liked me much—but then he said, "Nina wasn't the only one who argued with the old... with Frenetta yesterday."

"Gloria and Hildy did, too? About what?"

"Something about the house," Chip said. "I think they expected her to sell it to them."

"And she didn't want to?"

He shrugged.

I glanced at Rafe, who shrugged, too.

"I don't see how killing her would get them the house," I said. "Not unless they think they'll inherit." And unless they were related to Frenetta, I didn't see how they would.

Chip snorted. "I didn't say they killed her. I just said they argued with her."

"So who do you think killed her?"

He glanced at Nina. "It wasn't us."

"I didn't say it was," I said. "I just thought you might have some idea. You spent a couple days with her. We never even met her."

"You could have killed her before you knocked on the door last night," Chip said.

I stared at him. "Excuse me?"

"We heard your car drive into the lot and park. And then we heard your voices. And it was at least five minutes after that, that you knocked on the door and Nina went down and let you in. You had time to go up the stairs to the garage and smother the old lady, and then come back down."

"That's crazy. We never even met her. Why would we kill her?"

"Why would anyone?" Chip said. "And I didn't say you did. I just said you could have. You did something during that time. And I don't think you were standing in the parking lot."

"We went to look at the ocean," I said.

"It was dark," Chip answered.

"I know it was dark. We couldn't actually see it. But we didn't know that until we tried."

"So you say," Chip said and drained his beer. "But you can't prove it, can you?"

"We didn't meet anybody, if that's what you mean. But we were together. Can you prove where you were?"

"With Nina," Chip said, with a glance at her.

"Except for when Nina was downstairs letting us in."

"There wasn't enough time to run downstairs and out the front door and around the house and up the stairs to the apartment to smother the old lady and get back to bed before Nina got back upstairs," Chip said, in the tone of one who had tried it and failed.

Grudgingly, I had to admit he had a point. We hadn't spent that much time talking to Nina. And we'd heard the bedsprings squeak when we reached the second floor, so they'd been back at it by then.

Then again, it's possible for a single person to make bedsprings squeak, and make the bed knock against the wall. Granted, I was pretty sure we'd heard two voices, but I was willing to give that the benefit of the doubt, since I didn't like Chip. If I had to pin the murder on someone in the B and B, I'd rather have it be Chip than anyone else. I didn't know Vonnie and Groot very well, although I didn't dislike them, and I liked Gloria and Hildy well enough. If anyone in the house had murdered Frenetta, I wanted it to be Chip.

SEVEN

As soon as the waitress came back with our drinks and menus, Chip and Nina left. Nina hadn't even finished her beer when Chip dragged her away. And I don't think she wanted to leave, because she was looking over her shoulder as she went. It might have been the beer, but I think it was probably Rafe who was the draw.

We glanced at the menus—there were only a half dozen items to choose from—and then Rafe ordered a shrimp po'boy with onion rings, and I had to settle for a chicken sandwich with shoestring potatoes, since there was no roast beef to be had.

The waitress took our orders and the menus, and I turned to Rafe. "Do you think he did it?"

"Chip?"

I nodded.

"Dunno," Rafe said.

"What about Nina? Do you think she did it?"

He shook his head.

"Why not?"

He shrugged. I sniffed. "Let me guess. It's because she's blonde and pretty with big breasts."

"Is she?" He smiled. "I didn't notice."

"Sure." I rolled my eyes. "When she's forty, she's going to look sixty-five, you know."

He didn't answer, and I added, "You said the police think

Frenetta was drugged before she was killed, right?"

He nodded.

"Does that mean whoever killed her wanted to be sure she couldn't fight back?"

"It's possible," Rafe said.

"That might mean a woman did it. Not that that's very helpful. Other than Groot and Chip—and you—everyone in the house is a woman."

"Groot's old," Rafe said. "Older than Frenetta by a couple years, at least. He might could prefer that she wasn't in a position to fight back."

"Chip wouldn't care," I said. "He's young. Big. And looks strong. Or at least not wimpy. Between the two of you, you could probably take him with one hand tied behind your back. But he'd be plenty strong enough to smother an old woman."

Rafe didn't deny that he could annihilate Chip with one hand tied behind his back. Instead he just said, "If a woman killed her, most likely the drugs in the wine was to keep her from fighting back. But a man coulda killed her and just wanted to avoid the fight, too. It's hard to make murder look natural."

I'd take his word for it, because I wasn't about to ask how he knew. I was going to continue the conversation, though, when I voice said, "Mind if I join you?"

The voice was female. So was the speaker. Very much so.

Here was someone middle age had treated very well, indeed. I put her above forty, maybe closer to forty-five, but she had the toned body of a woman twenty years younger. I wished I looked as good, even when I wasn't pregnant. She was dressed in skin-tight jeans and a tank-top, one that emphasized toned arms and a very nice—natural—pair of breasts. The face was natural, too: high cheekbones, full lips, and big blue eyes with long lashes, under platinum blond hair—also natural, best as I could see—pulled straight back into a heavy chignon at the back of her head.

It should have made her look prim. The first time Rafe and I went on a date, I'd styled my hair like that, the better to indicate that there'd be no hanky-panky going on. I'd dressed in a school-marm blouse and calf-length skirt for the same reason. It hadn't worked. Rafe had told me the clothes and hair was a turn-on, because it made him wonder what I'd look like without the clothes and with my hair down.

So much for that plan.

Anyway, this gorgeous—slightly older—woman stood next to the table, grinning down at us—or at Rafe. I started to bristle, and was about to set her straight, when Rafe told her, "Sure, Sheriff. Have a seat."

Sheriff? This was the sheriff whose office he'd spent the afternoon in?

She grinned at me. "You must be the wife. Good to meet you."

She held out a hand. I took it, because it would be rude not to. "Savannah Martin. Collier."

"Tallulah Engebretsen. You can call me Lou."

Or maybe I'd just call her 'Sheriff,' the way Rafe did. "What can we do for you?"

"I saw you sitting here," Sheriff Engebretsen said easily, "and figured I'd introduce myself."

"Uh-huh. I suppose you were here with someone else, and he or she just left? Maybe right behind Chip and Nina?"

Rafe chuckled. The sheriff looked a bit chagrined. "Something like that."

"So you're following us? Why? We didn't have anything to do with Frenetta's death. We never even met her."

"So your husband told me," Lou Engebretsen said, with a glance at him. "If it makes you feel better, I've got people on all y'all, to make sure nobody tries to leave town before I figure this out."

That did make me feel better, actually.

"Are you any closer?"

"We've pretty much eliminated the two of you," the sheriff said. "The sleeping pills were in the wine. It was a new bottle. She opened it after dinner, and had a glass while she was preparing breakfast for this morning. The bottle was in the kitchen during that time, and people came and went. Anyone in the house might have added something to it."

"Except Rafe and me," I said. "We were still in Alabama at dinner-time."

"And that's why I've pretty much eliminated you," the sheriff answered.

'Pretty much' was better than nothing. "So was it one of the other guests?"

"It seems likely," Lou said. "None of the locals have come forward to say they were in the B and B last night. And none of the guests reported seeing any strangers."

"So I guess the guests are trying to blame each other?"

"The ladies from Boston are blaming Chip," Lou said. "Chip's blaming everybody but himself. And Vonnie thinks it was a natural death."

"Any chance it was?"

Lou shook her head. "Doesn't look that way. After cleaning up the kitchen, Frenetta took the bottle up to her apartment and finished it. It was still there this morning. Empty. And we can tell, from the residue in both the bottle and glass, that someone added a sleeping medication to it. In the form of ground-up pills, most likely."

Not much chance that was accidental, no. "Could she have done it herself?"

"I wouldn't think so," Lou said. "Most sleeping pills don't mix well with alcohol. And she wasn't stupid. She would have taken one or the other, but not both."

"Unless she was suicidal. She wasn't, was she?"

"If she was, no one's mentioned it," Lou said.

"The pills didn't kill her," Rafe added, "even mixed with the alcohol. The mixture just knocked her out."

"And then someone went upstairs and smothered her."

Lou nodded. "We're not sure if she left her door unlocked or whether her murderer had a key. Or whether she let someone in."

"Surely she wouldn't have gone to sleep with someone there."

"Depends on who it was," Lou said. "If it was her sister..."

"Sister?"

"Vonnie," Lou said.

"Vonnie is Frenetta's sister?"

"Yes," Lou said. "Why?"

Why? Well, first of all because I hadn't known. And then— "I guess I'm just surprised she left it to us to check on Frenetta this morning. If it was my sister who didn't come down to breakfast, I would be the first one up those stairs."

Of course, I was a perky twenty-eight, at least when I wasn't carrying ten extra pounds of baby. Vonnie was older. Mid-sixties, at least. Maybe she had a hard time getting around. So far I'd only seen her sitting down. For all I knew, she was in a wheelchair.

"Frenetta and Vonnie didn't always get along," Lou said.

"Why not?" Bad blood might be a good reason for murder.

"When Mrs. Wallin died," Lou said, and added, "Frenetta and Vonnie's mother—"

I nodded.

"—she left the house to Frenetta. Vonnie had married and moved to Tallahassee by then, and Frenetta was the one who stayed in Davenport and took care of her mother. I guess the old lady figured Vonnie didn't need the house, but Frenetta would be taken care of if she had it."

That made sense. "So what happened?"

"Vonnie tried to contest the will and lost. Frenetta turned the place into a B and B and ran it on her own. The sisters didn't speak for years. Maybe decades. It's only been in the past year or so that Vonnie and her husband have been coming back here."

"That's sad." Good that they had made up, I guess, before it was too late. But sad that the sisters had lost so much time together, and wouldn't have any more, now that Frenetta was gone.

Lou shrugged. "Anyway, the sleeping medicine in the wine would have been enough to knock Frenetta out, but not enough to kill her. And if she'd smothered herself, I would have expected you to find her facedown in the pillows. But you didn't."

Rafe shook his head. "She was lying on her left side. Blankets up to her shoulders, dressed in a nightgown, with a pillow under her head and another on the floor next to her. No sign of a struggle."

He had noticed a lot more about the crime scene than I had. I had seen Frenetta curled up on her side, with a blanket over her, but I hadn't noticed the nightgown or the second pillow.

"There was saliva on the pillowcase," Lou said.

"Maybe she drooled." I do sometimes. Not that I like to admit it.

Rafe hid a smile.

"This was the pillow on the floor," Lou said. "Not the one under her head. Someone placed that pillow over her face and held it there, and then dropped it on the floor when she was dead."

"Or she knocked it off the bed herself."

Rafe shook his head. "She was dead to the world, darlin'. Probably didn't stir at all after she crawled into bed."

Fine. "So someone went up to the apartment and smothered her. And it was one of the people in the B and B. Either before Rafe and I got there, or after."

She could have been asleep as easily as dead when we arrived in the parking lot at ten o'clock.

"That's about the strength of it," Lou agreed.

"Why? I never met her, but she was an elderly innkeeper in a small town in Florida. Who'd want her dead? Was she rich?"

"Not as far as I know," Lou said, "although I expect the

property is worth a pretty penny."

I expected she was right. Beachfront property isn't my specialty—Tennessee is landlocked, although houses and building lots on the river or lake go for a nice chunk of change—but it didn't take expertise to see that the Davenport Inn B and B was a beautiful, old house on a large piece of land across the street from the beach, and there are only so many of those around.

"I heard rumors that a developer was sniffing around last year sometime," Lou added. "Nothing ever came of it, that I know. People in Davenport are resistant to change. Nobody wants the town to become another Destin or Panama City Beach. We like it peaceful. But I remember there was talk about some developer in Atlanta making an offer."

Those Atlanta developers are everywhere. They're buying up large chunks of Nashville, too. Just a couple of months ago, a sub shop on West End Avenue, that had been there for forty years, had had to close its doors after an Atlanta developer bought the land. The plan was to raze the old building and put up a thirty-story apartment tower. And while that would mean more homes—or condos—for yours truly to buy and sell, I still wasn't thrilled about it. I'd only been in Nashville for eight years: three at Vanderbilt University, two with Bradley after I dropped out to marry him, and these last three on my own... but I'd already seen a lot of changes, and not all of them for the better.

Progress is necessary, and sometimes even good, but I don't think we have to lose everything old and original in the name of it. The idea of Frenetta's B and B being knocked down to make room for highrise apartment buildings with parking garages and pools and a view of the ocean from the thirtieth floor, gave me a bad taste in my mouth.

"Chip and Nina live in Atlanta," I said.

"That's what they said."

"Gloria and Hildy said they overheard Nina arguing with

Frenetta yesterday morning. About Chip."

"So they told me," Lou nodded.

"Do you think Chip did it? Is that why you're following him?"

"I'm not following him. David's following him. I'm following you."

Right. "Did you ask him what he does for a living? Chip?"

"I don't think he does anything," Lou said, "but Nina's father is a developer."

"Land developer?"

She nodded.

"That's quite a coincidence." What were the chances that last year's developer from Atlanta and Nina's father were one and the same?

"We're looking into it," Lou said. "The land the B and B sits on is worth a fortune. And a fortune's a good motive for murder. However—"

I nodded. This was something I knew about. "It isn't like Chip will get the land now that Frenetta is dead. I guess it goes to Vonnie, unless Frenetta had a will."

"She had a safety deposit box at the bank," Lou said. "I'll be checking it tomorrow morning. I'll also be checking with the local attorneys, once they open for business. But if there's no will, then yes, I assume Vonnie will get the house. Frenetta never did have any children."

"Nice for Vonnie, getting the house after all."

"It was thirty years ago," Lou said. "I'm sure she's over it by now. And as far as I know, she and her husband have a very nice house of their own in Tallahassee. They don't need this one."

"Did you make sure of that?"

She refrained from rolling her eyes, but I could tell she wanted to. "Yes, Mrs. Collier. We did. Financially, they're doing just fine."

Rafe chuckled. "Leave the sheriff be, darlin'. She knows how to do her job."

I'm sure she did. I was just used to bouncing ideas off Tamara Grimaldi, and I guess I'd gotten a little carried away. "Sorry."

"No problem." She got to her feet. "I see your food coming. I'll leave you alone to enjoy it. Don't leave town without letting me know."

She walked away without waiting for an answer. She and the waitress slithered around one another halfway to the door, and then Lou disappeared inside, and the waitress stopped beside our table to drop off the po'boy and chicken sandwich.

"That was interesting," I told Rafe after she'd walked away.

"What? Lou?" He was busy getting a good grip on his sandwich, and didn't even look up.

I nodded. "I'm no longer surprised they let you go this afternoon. You didn't mention that the sheriff was female."

"No reason to." He lifted the po'boy and took a bite. Remoulade oozed out and decorated the corners of his mouth. I smiled.

"It explains a lot. Women like you. You said so yourself."

He shrugged. "As long as *you* like me, that's all I care about. Eat your food, darlin'. You gotta build up your strength for later."

That sounded promising. I lifted the sandwich and took a bite. It was good, but the compulsion to speculate was too strong. I put it down again and picked up a fry. "I didn't know Vonnie was Frenetta's sister." *Nibble, nibble, nibble.* "Did you?"

The fries were good, too.

Rafe shook his head. "The only time I saw Vonnie and her husband, was this morning at breakfast. And a lot of old ladies look alike."

They do. Frenetta probably hadn't looked like herself when we saw her. Corpses rarely do, I've found. And it stood to reason that if she didn't look like herself, she wouldn't look like Vonnie, either.

"What do you think of the real estate angle?"

Rafe chewed and swallowed. "For someone who said she was starving, you sure ain't eating much."

"Sorry." I picked up another fry and put it in my mouth. "But what do you think?"

"I think it's none of our business," Rafe said. "I think Lou's capable of figuring it out without our help. And I think you oughta eat your dinner so I can take you back to the room and have my way with you."

"That's fine. But I'd still like to talk about who killed Frenetta and why."

"Married less than forty-eight hours," Rafe said, "and you're already tired of me?"

"I'll never get tired of you. But it's not like we can do anything about it now. We're here."

At the Sandbar. Not in the privacy of our own room at the B and B.

Rafe shook his head. "Fine. Talk about Frenetta."

"Well..." Now that I had permission, I wasn't quite sure what to say. "Someone killed her. And tried to pin it on us. I don't think it's a coincidence that, as soon as we left the house to go up to the apartment above the garage this morning, someone called the cops. They wanted us to be discovered standing over the body. I think it was Chip."

"It mighta been Chip," Rafe said, still enjoying his sandwich.

I took another bite of mine. Chewed and swallowed. "Lou said a real estate developer from Atlanta is trying to buy Frenetta's property. Nina's father is a developer. Gloria and Hildy said Nina and Frenetta argued about Chip yesterday. Nina said something to the effect that Frenetta better do right by Chip, or else."

Rafe nodded, his mouth full of shrimp.

"What do you want to bet Chip is here to try to convince Frenetta to sell the property to Nina's dad?"

Rafe swallowed. "That could be. But killing her ain't gonna

get him the property."

No, it wasn't. "Could it have been an accident? Maybe the sleeping pills in the wine really did kill her. Maybe Chip did it so he could get her to sign on the dotted line while she was groggy and didn't know what she was agreeing to, but then she died?"

Rafe shook his head. "Saliva on the pillow," he reminded me.

Right. I thought about it some more while I had a few fries and another bite of the chicken. "So maybe Chip put the sleeping pills in the drink, but someone else killed her."

"I thought you wanted it to be Chip."

"I do want it to be Chip. It just doesn't make any sense for it to be Chip."

Rafe shook his head. "You gonna finish those fries?"

There were a lot of them, so no. "Help yourself." I took another bite of the sandwich. "Who do you think did it?"

"Dunno," Rafe said, reaching for my fries. "Don't care."

"How can you not care?"

"Very easily." He popped a couple of fries in his mouth. "We didn't know her. We don't know any of the others. And figuring it out is somebody else's job. I'm on my honeymoon."

"That's never stopped you before."

"I've never been on my honeymoon before," Rafe said. "All I wanna do is have a good time and a lot of sex. Let Lou worry about it."

"But doesn't it bother you that we're sleeping in a house with a murderer?"

"We slept in a house with a murderer last night, too," Rafe said.

"But we didn't know about it then!"

"Right."

I blinked at him, chagrined.

"You almost finished?" Rafe asked, polishing off my French fries.

"I guess." The sandwich was so big I couldn't eat all of it. And

I had very few fries left.

He dug a couple of bills out of his pocket and tucked them under his empty glass—enough to cover the bill and a tip—and got up. "You wanna walk on the beach?"

Obviously he did. "Sure." I put my napkin down and got to my feet, as well. He took my hand and led me across the deck and down the stairs to the sand.

EIGHT

It was a nice evening. Not overcast like yesterday. The moon was out, and the sky speckled with stars. The waves lapped gently against the shore. We couldn't really see the ocean, but we could hear it. Rafe's hand was warm and hard around mine.

"When I retire," he told me, "I wanna live on the beach."

"I'm sure we can manage that." We had thirty years or so to save up, after all. And it would probably take all of that, but if beach living was what he wanted, I'd do everything I could to give it to him. So what if I'd have to spend my declining years under an umbrella?

He squeezed my hand. "You still gonna wanna be married to me when I'm old and bald with a metal detector and a sun hat, digging tin cans and wedding bands outta the sand?"

"That depends," I said. "Are you still going to want to be married to me when I have wrinkles and gray hair?"

"I've seen your mama, darlin'," Rafe told me. "You ain't got nothing to worry about. When you're sixty, you're still gonna look forty-five. And gorgeous."

I hoped he was right.

"And anyway, I didn't marry you 'cause you look good."

"You married me because you knocked me up and my brother came after you with a shotgun."

"No," Rafe said. "He didn't even warn me I'd better do right by you."

"Figures."

He grinned, his teeth white in the darkness. "Your brother ain't stupid. He knows I'm crazy about you. I'll stick around as long as you'll have me. And I ain't doing nothing to change your mind so you'll kick me out early."

"You don't have to worry about that." I rubbed my cheek against his shoulder. "I'll keep you as long as you want to stay. Hopefully we'll both be ninety-five before either of us has to worry about it."

"I'll drink to that." He dropped my hand to drape his arm over my shoulders and pull me closer. "How're you liking married life so far?"

"I like it just fine," I said. "Although I'd like it better if our hostess hadn't gotten murdered."

"And here we go again."

"I'm sorry. I just can't stop thinking about it. Someone in the B and B is a murderer. We'll be sleeping next door to a killer tonight."

"We slept next door to a killer last night, too." He shook his head before we could start rehashing the conversation we'd already had. "I'll protect you."

"I'm not worried that he's going to do anything to me," I said. And added, "Or she," just to be fair.

"Then you'd better stop asking questions, darlin'. You know the second victim's always the one who knows too much."

"I'll be safe, then. I don't know anything."

"Maybe you do," Rafe said, "but you don't realize it."

I shook my head. "I don't think so. I think I'm safe. But feel free to stay close all night to make sure."

"I think I might could do that," Rafe said, and kept walking.

We made it back to the B and B without running into anything worse than a jogger, another couple walking hand in hand, and a guy who looked like he was preparing to spend the night on the beach, but didn't want us to realize it. It was probably illegal.

Back at the Davenport Inn, it looked like business as usual. Not that we'd been there before and had anything to compare it to, but nothing seemed amiss. Nina and Chip were still out, or might be upstairs in their room, but Gloria and Hildy, Vonnie and Groot were downstairs in the parlor, watching *Dancing with the Stars* and critiquing the moves while sipping drinks.

When we walked in, they all turned to us.

"Oh," Gloria said after a moment, "it's you."

"Did you expect someone else?"

She hesitated. "We thought maybe the sheriff had news."

"We just spoke to her," I said. "At the Sandbar. She isn't ready to make an arrest yet."

Groot muttered something, and I added, "Excuse me?"

"I said, what's she doing at the Sandbar if there's a murderer to find?"

"Following those of us who are suspects to make sure we don't leave town," I said.

He smirked. "Are you a suspect?"

"We're all suspects," Hildy told him, before I could say that no, I wasn't, because we'd gotten to Davenport too late to have doctored the wine. "Someone killed her, and we were right here."

"And she was out there," Groot said, pointing to the wall, behind which lay the kitchen, and then the parking lot and the garage. "Anyone coulda walked up those steps and smothered her."

"But only the people who had access to the house could have put the sleeping pills in the wine," Hildy said.

The sheriff must have told her that. They'd been asked questions about the wine bottle and who'd had access to it, I assumed.

Groot muttered something, but not out loud.

"Here you go." Vonnie put what looked like a mint julep in my hand, and handed another to Rafe. Playing hostess, I guess, in the absence of her sister. "Have a seat."

"Thank you." I sank down on one of the chintz sofas and put my glass on the table in front of me, since I couldn't drink it. Rafe sat down beside me and took a sip of his. His face twisted. Too much sugar, I guess. To sweet, for someone whose preferred beverage is beer.

I turned back to Vonnie, who had resumed her seat next to Groot on the other side of the table. "The sheriff said Frenetta was your sister. I didn't realize. I'm sorry for your loss."

She blinked. I guess she hadn't expected condolences. Or maybe hadn't expected anyone here to know about the relationship.

"This is a beautiful house," I added, glancing around the parlor. Eleven foot ceilings, eight foot windows, tiled fireplace. "The sheriff said you grew up here?"

Vonnie nodded.

"We live in an old Victorian house in Nashville. Rafe's grandmother's house. It was probably built around the same time as this one."

I glanced at Rafe. He glanced back at me. I returned my attention to Vonnie. "And I'm a real estate agent. I've seen a lot of these old houses. This one is lovely. And very nicely maintained. Lots of original features."

"I'm not interested in selling," Vonnie said.

Gloria and Hildy exchanged a look, and it took me a second to find my voice. "I didn't think you were." And anyway, I would never be so uncouth as to suggest it, when her sister wasn't even in the ground yet. Making a sales pitch hadn't been my intention at all. I'd been leading up to something else. "Although the sheriff did mention that she'd heard rumors that a developer from Atlanta was interested in buying."

Vonnie's lips tightened. "That won't happen."

"But is it true, though? Someone was trying to buy the place? Was your sister interested in selling?"

"No," Vonnie said. "This is our home. It's been in our mother's family for three generations."

Gloria and Hildy exchanged another look, but neither spoke.

"What will you do with the house now? The two of you live in Tallahassee, right? Will you move back here, or hire someone to keep running the place?"

"We haven't talked about it," Vonnie said, in a frosty tone.

She obviously didn't want to talk about it. And I'm not one to push in where I'm not wanted. "Well, it's a lovely place. I wish you the best with it." I got to my feet and glanced at my husband. "I guess we'll go upstairs now."

Rafe nodded and took my hand. "We'll see y'all in the morning."

"Good night," Gloria said, and Hildy smiled, sort of motherly and with that twinkle in her eye that said she knew exactly what we'd be doing in the privacy of our room. The old me would have been embarrassed. The new me was on her honeymoon, and didn't care that everyone knew we were headed upstairs to make love.

"Breakfast at eight," Gloria threw after us as we headed for the stairs.

I glanced at her over my shoulder, and she added, "The food's just sitting there. We may as well eat it. We're stuck here until the police informs us we can leave. And I don't mind cooking."

"That's very kind of you."

She shrugged. "Someone's gotta do it."

True. It would have been more suitable for Vonnie to step up, I guess, but maybe she didn't like to cook. And with what had happened, making sure that Frenetta's guests were comfortable—when she probably wished we were anywhere but here—wasn't likely to be a priority, anyway.

"We'll be sure to come down early," I said, and then we headed out the door and up the stairs to our room.

I'll spare you the details of the next thirty minutes. We walked into the room and locked the door behind us. Rafe kissed me, and one thing led to another. Thirty minutes later, we were side by side under the covers.

"Did that strike you as a little weird?" I asked when we'd caught our collective breaths.

"What?"

He sounded groggy. Men do after sex, I've discovered, although he doesn't usually drop off this fast. Might be the beer in combination with a lot of sun earlier today.

I turned my head to look at him. He looked OK, just tired. "All of it. Vonnie jumping to the conclusion that I was offering to buy the house. Gloria making breakfast. Why isn't Vonnie making breakfast? Gloria is a guest."

"Not everybody likes to cook," Rafe muttered, halfway to dreamland, "and I'm sure Vonnie just wants to pretend we ain't here."

No doubt. "We are, though. We are guests in what's now her house, and good manners dictate that she make us feel at home." Even if we were only here because the police wouldn't let us leave.

"Her sister died," Rafe said. "She's prob'ly got other things on her mind."

No doubt. Maybe I was reading too much into the situation. Maybe Gloria had simply noticed that Vonnie was overwhelmed by her sister's death, and had taken it upon herself to play breakfast cook.

Vonnie hadn't struck me as particularly overwhelmed—let alone grief-stricken—but let's face it, some people are very reserved. It isn't proper to wail and cry in public. Vonnie might be mourning inside; we just couldn't see it.

I could hear a murmur of voices from downstairs, where they were still watching TV and talking. Closer by, it was quiet. Nina and Chip must still be out, because there was no sound from their room. The bed wasn't banging against the wall, the springs weren't squeaking, and Chip wasn't snoring. Rafe was starting to fall asleep, though, his breaths becoming slow and even. His eyelashes were long and thick, like fans against his cheeks, and his lips were softer in sleep than when he's awake.

He's beautiful. And I love him so much it hurts. Tomorrow was supposed to be our last day here. I'd make sure he got to spend as much of it as possible on the beach. With no interruptions by the sheriff or anybody else. I'd take a couple of the Barbara Botticelli books with me, and spend the day under the umbrella. He could enjoy the beach and the ocean as much as he wanted, until he got sunburned and sick of it.

And hopefully, the day after that, we'd be allowed to go home. With so few suspects, all under one roof—a roof that had belonged to the victim—surely the sheriff would figure out whodunit soon, and let us all go. I mean, how hard could it be?

It wasn't Rafe or me. We'd gotten here too late to doctor the wine, and we didn't know Frenetta, so we had no motive.

Chip and Nina had only been here for a day when Frenetta died. Normally, that would let them out. They hadn't known her long enough to want to kill her. Not enough history.

But there are exceptions to that rule. One of them could have known her from before. Or she might have known a secret about one of them—like, Chip had lived in Davenport before, and he had embezzled money or was generally suspected of having killed an earlier girlfriend. And when Frenetta threatened to tell Nina about it, Chip killed her to keep her quiet.

That's the kind of thing that happens in books and movies. Not so much in real life. If Chip had lived in Davenport before— and especially if he'd committed a crime—the sheriff would have know about it.

No, if he and/or Nina were guilty, it was much more likely to have something to do with the real estate angle, and Nina's father. Maybe Chip had been trying to impress Nina's dad by convincing Frenetta to sell her property, and he'd gotten a little carried away, and Frenetta had ended up dead. Chip struck me as the kind of idiot who'd think forcing someone to sign sale papers would be a good idea.

Gloria and Hildy, by their own account, had been here twice before, over the course of a year. They'd had enough time to get to know Frenetta. One or both of them might have had a reason to kill her. I hadn't met the woman, so I didn't know how frustrating she'd been to deal with, but she might have been driving everyone around her crazy.

And of course Vonnie had known her their whole lives, and Groot for thirty or forty years, depending on how long he and Vonnie had been married. Plenty of time to get on each other's nerves.

Catherine had met Frenetta when she, Jonathan, and the kids had been here before. Maybe she could shed some light on just how objectionable the dead woman had been, and whether her personality had been something that might have made people want to kill her.

At the very least, I should probably tell her what had happened. I'd been planning to do it yesterday, but then I'd forgotten.

Rafe was deeply asleep by now, and I didn't want to wake him, so I slipped from the bed as quietly as I could, and pulled the sundress back over my head. Then I grabbed my phone from my purse and tiptoed across to the door and out.

The others were still downstairs. I could hear their voices better from the landing. Groot's low grumble, Gloria's pleasant alto, Hildy's higher-pitched gurgle, and an occasional stiff comment from Vonnie.

I couldn't hear Chip or Nina, and there was no sound from behind their door, not even when I put my ear to it.

The temptation to try the knob was too much. It turned in my hand, silently. I pushed the door open and peeked in.

Should I risk turning on a lamp?

I decided I should.

The light illuminated a room in disarray. Unmade bed, bureau drawers hanging open, closet door standing ajar.

I'd have suspected a burglary if not for one thing: there was nothing here. No clothes in the closet or in any of the drawers. No shoes on the floor, no toiletries in the attached bathroom, no suitcase or other personal belongings at all.

Looked like our conversation at the Sandbar had spooked Chip and Nina. They'd gone home and packed up their stuff and hightailed it out of Davenport. I wondered how far they'd gone before David Chang had stopped them.

This probably put the final nail in Chip's coffin. Why would he run if he hadn't killed Frenetta, after all? But I was here, alone, with a chance to snoop in everyone else's rooms while they were downstairs. It seemed too good an opportunity to waste.

I crossed the landing on tiptoe.

Vonnie and Groot's door was unlocked, as well.

I hesitated, peeling my ears for sounds from below and the indication that anyone was coming upstairs. Everything was quiet. The TV was still on in the parlor.

I pushed the door open and took a couple of careful steps inside the room.

It looked a lot like ours. Same bright color scheme, same fun island-type furnishings. The bed was unmade, and on the rumpled comforter sat an open suitcase, half full. I guess maybe Vonnie and Groot had been on their way back to Tallahassee this morning, and their leaving had been derailed by the death.

The attached bathroom was white, with palm trees on the shower curtain. (Ours was sand-colored with sea stars, in case you wondered.) There was a toiletries bag sitting on the back of the toilet. I felt like I had already spent too much time in here, but I tiptoed over and peeked in. The usual array of creams and hair brushes greeted me, along with a couple of medicine bottles, of the prescription and non-prescription kind. I guess when folks get older, they get more aches and pains.

I wanted to dig through and see what the various pills were for—whether any of them were sleeping medicines—but the police had already been through the B and B. I had noticed a slight disarray in our stuff when I came home yesterday afternoon. They would have checked the medications. Lou Engebretsen wasn't stupid.

Then again, Groot and Vonnie didn't strike me as stupid, either. If one of their medications had been used to kill Frenetta, it wouldn't be sitting here in plain sight.

I tiptoed back out and closed the door gently behind me. There was no activity on the stairs or landing, and the TV was still droning.

I moved a couple of steps to my left, and tried the last door.

The knob turned, and the door opened. I ducked into Gloria and Hildy's room for a quick look around.

It was painted tropical pink, and I took a moment to be abjectly grateful that Frenetta hadn't given it to me and Rafe. It was a little like being stuck inside a giant Pepto-Bismol bottle.

Other than that, it looked like our room, and like Vonnie and Groot's. Frenetta must have gotten a buy-one, get-one deal on white wicker furniture when she put the place together.

In here, the bed was neatly made and everything was in its place. Gloria and Hildy must not be planning to move on, because there was no suitcase in sight. Maybe they had booked the whole summer.

Wonder whether Vonnie would kick them out early?

The bedside table on the left had a paperback on it. Not a Botticelli. Gloria—or maybe Hildy—liked thrillers. The cover had a picture of a small dark figure inside a tunnel, along with one of those generic thriller titles in big letters. *Payback* or *Runaway* or *Malice*.

Under the book was a sheaf of papers. I lifted the book and peered down.

It was a legal contract, for the transfer of property. The address of the B and B was written on the property line, and the price was a cool million and a half. The parties to the contract were Gloria Duncan and Hildy McLeod as the buyers, Frenetta Wallin as seller. The contract date was three days ago.

I flipped to the last page, and the signatures.

Gloria's and Hildy's were there, duly notarized. So was Frenetta's.

Before I had time to process the information, let alone think through the repercussions of what it might mean—Frenetta was selling the B and B to Gloria and Hildy?—the door to the corridor opened with a faint squeak. I spun around to see a dark figure filling the doorway.

NINE

"I'll take that," Vonnie said, holding out her hand.

She wasn't actually filling the doorway. For a second, it just seemed like she did. It was probably the pistol in her hand.

"Where did you get that?" I couldn't take my eyes off it. It was huge and gray and looking down the barrel, I could almost see a bullet with my name on it.

I'd been shot once before. It hurts. When Vonnie wiggled the gun suggestively, I handed over the paperwork without demurring.

She glanced at the front page, and her mouth curved. "Thank you very much."

Very polite of her. I couldn't bring myself to return the favor and tell her she was welcome. "You didn't answer my question," I said instead.

"What...? Oh. Have you seen the crime rates in Tallahassee lately?" She shook her head. "The town's going to hell in a hand basket. Hoodlums everywhere, with guns and knives. You can't be too careful."

I guess you couldn't. "Is that why you killed your sister?" Because she had to have killed Frenetta, if she was up here with a gun. Why else would she be threatening me?

"I don't know what you mean," Vonnie said. "I caught you burglarizing one of my guest rooms."

Well, yes. Technically, she had. And technically, that was a defense of sorts.

"So you didn't kill your sister?"

"Why would I kill my sister?" Vonnie wanted to know.

"I don't know. Maybe because she was selling the house—this house, the one you both grew up in—and you didn't want her to?"

Her eyes flickered. I pressed the advantage I figured I had. "She got the house when your mother died. You didn't, even though you were the eldest."

Pure guesswork. I had no idea whether she was older than Frenetta or not, but I thought she might be, since she'd married first. At any rate, she didn't contradict me.

"Frenetta was always mother's favorite. Even when we were small. Mother always liked her better."

"You must have hated that," I said sympathetically, even as I wondered whether Mother liked Catherine better than me.

She probably did. Catherine hadn't gotten herself knocked up out of wedlock and ended up marrying Rafe Collier. Although if Mother had a favorite among her children, I was pretty sure it was Dix. I'm certain she liked Sheila, Dix's late wife, better than either me or Catherine.

But now wasn't the time to worry about that. I turned my attention back to Vonnie and the gun. "She shouldn't have treated you differently. You were sisters. Equal. But Frenetta got the house, and what did you get?"

"Nothing," Vonnie said through clenched teeth.

"It wasn't fair."

She shook her head. "And she didn't just live in it. She rented it out! Strangers, sleeping in my room!"

She directed a fulminating glance over my shoulder, into Gloria and Hildy's room. Gloria and Hildy must have been here already when Groot and Vonnie showed up, so Vonnie couldn't have her old room for the weekend.

"And then you realized she was thinking of selling."

"She called me," Vonnie said bitterly. "Out of the blue. We hadn't spoken to one another in years, and she calls to tell me a real estate developer had made an offer for the house and the land. She was going to sell *my* house, and for a lot of money!"

Good for her.

I didn't say it, since I figured the sentiment wouldn't go over well. I did endeavor to keep her talking, since the longer we stood here, the better the chances that someone would come up the stairs and see what was going on. Or that Rafe would wake up and notice I wasn't in bed, and come looking for me.

In fact, there might be something I could do about that. I still had my phone. I'd put it in my pocket before picking up the sales contract from the bedside table. It was still there. If I could speed-dial Rafe's phone by touch, without looking at the display, and wake him up...

I slipped a hand into the folds of my skirt, and from there into the pocket. To distract Vonnie, I used my other hand to point to the papers in her hand. "What's up with that? If a developer from Atlanta wanted to buy the place, what's that contract all about?"

"Everyone wanted to buy it!" Vonnie shrieked, practically frothing at the mouth. I kept my eyes on her, while inside my pocket, I was frantically trying to push the right buttons on the phone. Which, let me tell you, is a lot harder to do when you can't see what you're doing.

Eventually, I thought I had done it, and pressed the slick screen in the area where I thought I was making the call. And then I peeled my ears for the sound of Rafe's phone ringing in the other room.

I used to have my phone set to play the Hallelujah Chorus. That was last year. Now, I've programmed different ringtones for different people. Detective Grimaldi's is the theme from *Hawaii Five-O*. Mother's is a certain melody snipped from *The Wizard of Oz*, better left unnamed. And Rafe's is the wedding march, at least this week. Now that we were married, I should probably

JENNA BENNETT | 99

program something else.

If I ever got the chance.

This was a hell of a way to start married life. Being held at gunpoint during the honeymoon.

I listened for the sound of Mendelssohn from across the hall, but heard nothing.

Dammit, if not Rafe, who had I called?

Or maybe I hadn't called anybody. Maybe I'd just started a scroll through my images, or an ebook, or something like that.

But just in case someone was listening, I kept the phone on. If Vonnie shot me and buried my body in the sand, at least someone would know what happened. I had no way of knowing who, but somebody.

"You sister signed that." I pointed to the contract. "She sold the house. So why did you say that you wouldn't? It's already done."

"Not after I burn the contract," Vonnie said. "Then it'll be their word against mine. And without my sister's signature, what can they do?"

Not a whole lot, I imagined. If Vonnie had possession of the house, and Gloria and Hildy didn't have possession of the contract, they might not be able to do anything. Unless there was another copy somewhere.

"So you killed your sister so she wouldn't sell the house," I said. "When did you find out that she'd sold it already?"

Vonnie looked like she was grinding her teeth, but the gun didn't waver. "I thought I was stopping her from agreeing to sell the house to that little rat Chip. She kept saying no, but I was afraid, sooner or later, she'd give in. She always wanted children—" her expression said that she couldn't imagine why, "and he was ingratiating himself. He could be charming when he wanted to be."

Her expression was grim. I'd take her word for it, although you couldn't prove it by me. I hadn't seen anything remotely resembling charm in Chip.

"And when you thought she might give in, you killed her."

There was a sound in the hallway, and I glanced that way. Vonnie smiled unpleasantly. "Don't get any ideas about someone coming to save you. Chip and Nina are gone. Groot is keeping the ladies occupied downstairs. He'll make sure they don't come up here. And I've taken care of your husband."

A chill crept down my spine. "What do you mean," I asked, and it took effort to keep my voice steady, "you've taken care of him?"

"A couple of pills in the mint julep," Vonnie said with a shrug, "and he'll be sleeping like a baby." Her eyes turned angry again when she looked at me. "You were supposed to drink, too. But you didn't."

"I'm pregnant," I said. Maybe it would make her think twice about shooting me.

Then again, she hadn't thought twice about killing her own sister, so probably not.

"That's too bad."

Yes, it was. "What are you going to do with me? I mean, it isn't like my... my husband—" I stumbled over the word, "is going to believe that I walked out on him."

Rafe would never believe that. Just as, a week ago, when he didn't show up to our (first) wedding ceremony, I hadn't believed he'd walked out on me. Mother had been convinced he did. Everyone else had been open to the possibility, even if they'd had doubts.

I had refused to believe it.

Mostly.

And Rafe would absolutely refuse to believe I'd left him. He'd know I wouldn't.

But that wouldn't make me any less dead.

"I think you must have decided to take a walk on the beach," Vonnie said, "and unfortunately you got caught in a riptide."

"I see. And how do you plan to get me out of the house, past Gloria and Hildy, without them suspecting anything?"

"I'll leave that up to you," Vonnie told me, as she backed slowly through the doorway. "I imagine we'll be able to work something out."

The gun dropped a few inches, from my chest to my stomach. I put a hand on it, automatically. There was nothing my hand could do to protect the contents if she fired, but the threat was effective. Certainly enough to make me determined to draw as little attention to myself as possible on the way down the stairs.

Vonnie passed through the opening and into the hallway, and that's when it happened.

A banshee yell—or war cry—made me jump what felt like a foot in the air. Vonnie jumped too, and thankfully did not discharge the gun. A well-placed foot in a tennis shoe kicked it from her hand, and then a hundred and eighty pounds of irate female landed on Vonnie and knocked her flat. I heard her head hit the floor with a thunk. Luckily she managed to land on the hallway runner; if she'd hit the hardwood floor, she might not have gotten up again.

Not that she got up. Gloria landed on her and kept her down.

Yes, Gloria. Not Rafe. He was there, too, but not in any kind of position to subdue a suspect. He had to lean against the wall to keep upright, and his eyes were practically crossed. For once, sheer willpower was unequal to the task. I'd seen him sideline pain and fear and a lot of other things when necessarily, but Vonnie's sleeping pills had proven to be too much for him.

"I called Lou," he muttered, his eyelids at half mast.

I went over to him and put an arm around his waist. "Thank you."

He looked at me, but I'm not sure he saw me. Not clearly. "Got your call. Just couldn't save the day."

"It's OK. It all worked out." Hildy had Groot under control downstairs, I assumed, and Gloria was certainly on top of things here. Literally. "Let's go back to bed."

Even half asleep, he managed a grin. "Yes'm."

Gloria snorted, but it was a humorous sort of snort. She looked up at me and winked.

"And maybe we'll put some clothes on, too," I added.

Rafe blinked. Slowly. And peered down his own front. "Shit," he said.

"I know." I led him back toward the door to the bedroom, while he attempted—in vain—to cover his exposed parts with one hand. He has big hands, but not big enough for the task. "It's all right. I don't think Gloria cares. And you probably gave Vonnie a thrill."

"Did I give you a thrill, darlin'?"

"Always," I said, guiding him through the door. "Here we go. Just crawl back into bed. That's good..." I pulled the blanket over him. I think he was probably out cold by the time his head hit the pillow. I was frankly amazed that he'd managed to drag himself out of bed and out to the hallway in the condition he was. He'd even been coherent enough to call the sheriff. Or at least he'd managed to dial the number. Whether he'd made himself understood was another matter. God only knew what he'd told her.

Right on cue, there was a knock on the door downstairs. Gloria lifted her head, and Vonnie stirred feebly.

"I'll get it," I said, as a voice hollered, "Sheriff's deputy. Open the door!"

It took me thirty seconds to get down the stairs and through the house. By then, Lou Engebretsen was going crazy on the front porch. When I opened the door—and took a prudent step back—she burst into the foyer with gun drawn, sweeping the room from left to right before turning to me.

It took a second for her to recognize me, I think. At first, it looked like she didn't know who I was. Then her eyes cleared. "Good. You're alive."

I nodded.

"What's going on?"

"I was snooping," I said. With a grimace, since I figured I knew how the sheriff would feel about that. "Rafe fell asleep, and I went out in the hallway to call my sister." Whom I still hadn't called, incidentally. "I knew nobody was upstairs, so I tried Chip and Nina's door."

Lou tsked, but not in a serious way.

"They're gone. I assume you already know that?"

She nodded. "David caught up with them before they crossed the county line. They're cooling their heels in jail."

Good to know. However— "They actually didn't do it. I guess they just freaked out when they came under suspicion. Vonnie said that Chip had been trying to convince Frenetta to sell. I got the sense he might have used some undue pressure."

Lou nodded. "He admitted as much. But swore up and down he hadn't had anything to do with killing her. They both swore they'd been together all night, except for the few minutes when Nina came downstairs to open the door for you."

She hesitated a moment before she added, "They're still trying to blame you for it."

"We weren't here," I said. "And really, I should have figured it out a long time ago. Chip wouldn't have needed to drug Frenetta to kill her. He was a young, strong, big guy, and she was a smallish, older women. He could have twisted her neck and been done with it."

Lou nodded.

"Hildy is the follower in their relationship, and Gloria the leader. If one of them was going to kill Frenetta, it would be Gloria. And she's also big and strong. Bigger and stronger than Frenetta."

"Gym teacher," Lou said.

"I don't think she would have bothered with the sleeping pills, either. I also don't think she's the type."

"So who did it?"

"Vonnie," I said.

"*Vonnie?*"

"She's the only one of us who'd need Frenetta sedated in order to kill her. Not just because she's older than Frenetta, and probably weaker—Frenetta worked all day, every day, and Vonnie doesn't look like she does much except go to the hairdresser and have her nails done—but I'm sure she wouldn't want Frenetta awake and cognizant of what was going on while Vonnie killed her. They were sisters, after all."

Lou nodded. "Makes sense. Can you tell me why?"

"Frenetta wanted to sell the place," I said. "Vonnie didn't want her to."

"And that's why she killed her?"

"Frenetta wasn't interested in selling to Nina's father. But she had agreed to sell to Gloria and Hildy. My guess is, they wanted to keep the B and B as a B and B, and weren't going to develop the land. They told me they fell in love with the place the first time they came here."

"So what happened tonight? Your husband was asleep and you were snooping."

I nodded. "I didn't know until later, but Vonnie put something in his drink. When we came home from dinner earlier, all four of them were in the parlor watching TV and drinking mint juleps."

Lou glanced at the door to the parlor, from behind which we could still hear the sound of the TV.

"Vonnie gave us each a drink. I didn't drink any of mine, since..."

She nodded. "But your husband did?"

"He finished it. I think it tasted weird, though, because he grimaced. I figured it was just too sweet—he prefers beer—but now I wonder."

"So you went upstairs, and he fell asleep?"

"Eventually. We're on our honeymoon, as you know."

"Right," Lou drawled. "So he fell asleep, and you decided to snoop."

"I actually decided to call my sister. I was going to do it earlier, but I forgot. She was the one who booked us in here. She was here with her family once. I figured I ought to tell her what had happened." And pick her brain. But it was probably better not to mention that. "And I didn't want to disturb Rafe, so I got dressed again, and took my phone out on the landing. And then I had the idea to check whether the doors were locked."

"And what did you discover?"

"That Chip and Nina were gone. You already know that. That Vonnie and Groot have lots of medicine bottles in their toiletries bag. You probably know that, too."

She nodded.

"And in Gloria and Hildy's room, I found a purchase and sale contract between the two of them and Frenetta, for the B and B. Signed and ratified. I was looking at it when Vonnie came upstairs and found me. She had a gun."

Lou's eyes narrowed.

"She made me give her the paperwork. But when she backed out of the room, Gloria kicked the gun out of her hand and landed on her. I assume they're still upstairs."

"And Hildy and Groot?"

"In there," I said, pointing to the parlor. "Or so I assume. You knocked, and I didn't take the time to check."

"Leave it to me." She headed for the door.

I trailed behind, of course.

Yes, they were there. Groot red-faced and furious on the sofa, and Hildy standing over him, armed with a fireplace poker.

Lou took in the scene in a single glance. "You can put that down," she told Hildy. "Evening, Mr. Jenkins."

Hildy lowered the poker reluctantly. "He wanted to go upstairs and check on his wife."

"I'll go check on her in a minute," Lou said, at the same time as I told them, "She's fine. Gloria's on her."

Literally.

Lou glanced at me, but didn't say anything. "Just sit tight," she told Groot.

"I wanna see my wife!"

"I'll bring her down in a minute. Try to be patient 'till then."

She nodded to Hildy, who took a better grip on the fireplace poker and tried to look fierce.

I didn't think there was anything I could do upstairs, so when Lou went to the bottom of the staircase and headed up, I stayed where I was. "What happened down here?"

"As soon as you left," Hildy said with a grimace, "Gloria told Vonnie that it didn't matter whether she wanted to sell the house or not; it was already a done deal. Vonnie didn't like that. Gloria said she could prove it, that she had the paperwork upstairs on the bedside table. Vonnie said she'd go look for herself, since she was cold anyway, and wanted a sweater."

"Why didn't she leave the gun with Groot?"

"She didn't have a gun when she went upstairs," Hildy said. "She must have picked it up on the way."

And I hadn't even noticed her stopping off in her room. Some detective I was.

"When she didn't come back down," Hildy continued, "Gloria decided to go after her. Groot tried to stop her—he even got physical, and Gloria had to put him back in the chair—and then she gave me the fireplace poker and told me to keep him there. So I did."

She glanced at Groot, who glowered at her.

"They killed Frenetta," I said.

She nodded. "We figured that out."

Groot muttered something, and I turned to him. "What?"

He raised his voice. "It wasn't fair. She getting the house and Vonnie getting nothing."

"Maybe not. But it wasn't fair to kill her, either."

He had no response to that. Outside in the hallway, we could hear steps on the stairs. Lou came down with Vonnie in front of her, while Gloria made up the rear.

"C'mon, Mr. Jenkins," Lou said, herding Vonnie through the foyer. "Out to the car."

Groot heaved himself to his feet. "Where ya taking her?"

"Just over to the office so we can talk." She passed through the front door with Vonnie in front. Groot lumbered after.

"Do you need help?" I asked.

Lou shook her head. "We're fine. Stay here with your husband."

No problem. Although if Groot and Vonnie overpowered her on the way to the sheriff's office, I was totally going to remind her of this.

"I'll talk to y'all tomorrow." She closed the door. All that was left was silence, and a bit of an anticlimactic feeling. I looked at Gloria and Hildy. They looked back at me. I daresay we all looked a little shell-shocked.

"So you own the place," I said. It explained a lot. Or at least it explained why Gloria was making breakfast tomorrow. "Congratulations."

"It isn't ours yet. We haven't exchanged the money." She glanced at Hildy. "Now it might not be."

"It's all right." Hildy took Gloria's hand. "We still have the money. If it doesn't work out, we'll find another place to buy."

"I liked this one," Gloria said, but she leaned against Hildy, who leaned against her. I guess they needed the comfort.

Comfort sounded pretty nice, actually. In another minute, I intended to crawl under the covers with Rafe and be comforted, too. Even if he was dead to the world. But first—

"She might need to sell. I don't know how much money they have, but a good defense attorney doesn't come cheap. Not in a murder trial. And anyway, isn't there some rule about not benefitting from a crime?"

"I don't know," Gloria said, but she looked a little more cheerful. "I guess we'll have to look into it tomorrow."

"After we cook breakfast," Hildy reminded her.

"I'm going upstairs," I said. "I want to make sure Rafe is all right and is sleeping off the medicine."

They both nodded. "We'll see you tomorrow. Breakfast at eight."

"We'll be there," I promised, and headed for the stairs.

EPILOGUE

"Feel free to stay another night," Gloria told us over breakfast the next morning. "We intend to."

She exchanged a look with Hildy, who nodded. "As soon as it's business hours—ten o'clock hereabouts—we're calling the lawyers. The house is rightfully ours, and we intend to keep it."

I wished them luck. Hopefully Vonnie would be busy elsewhere and wouldn't have time to contest anything.

We were sitting across from one another at the dining room table, over a spread of pecan coffee cake—the one Frenetta had been preparing two days ago, I assumed—frittata, roasted potatoes, and some other things. Rafe was sucking down coffee like his life depended on it, and looked like he could use a couple of toothpicks to help keep his eyes open. He was hardly eating anything at all, just drooping over his plate.

"I don't think so," I said. "This hasn't been very relaxing. I think we'll just go on home and sleep in our own bed tonight." Where nobody was trying to poison or shoot us.

Hildy nodded sympathetically. "Maybe you can come down again sometime? Maybe after the baby's born?"

If the inn is still here. But I didn't say it. Didn't want to throw cold water on their parade, and was trying to keep a positive attitude. "Sure. Rafe enjoyed the ocean. It was just all the other stuff going on that was the problem."

They both nodded. "I don't understand how anyone can kill

someone over a house," Hildy said, with a shudder. "And not just anyone, but a sister."

I didn't either. And speaking of sisters, I still hadn't called mine.

Before I could pursue that thought, however, there was a knock on the door.

"I'll get it," Gloria said. Rafe barely even stirred, so hopefully whoever was outside, wasn't a threat.

Then again, the three of us had managed pretty well last night, so maybe that wouldn't be the end of the world.

We heard voices in the foyer, and then footsteps coming back toward us. Gloria came into the dining room followed by Lou Engebretsen.

The sheriff looked beat, like she hadn't slept much last night, and Hildy immediately went into hostess mode. "Have a seat, Sheriff Engebretsen. Coffee?"

"Don't mind if I do," Lou said and dropped down onto the nearest chair. Meanwhile, Hildy bustled about getting her a place setting and a cup of coffee.

"What's new, Sheriff?" Gloria asked.

Lou sighed. "Nothing. Just the same as was new last night."

"Did they confess?" I asked. "To killing Frenetta?"

"Vonnie did." She took the mug of coffee Hildy put in front of her and lifted it to her lips for a swallow. "Thank you."

"You're welcome." Hildy sat back down beside Gloria. "That's good, right? That she admitted it?"

Lou nodded, her eyes a little clearer as the coffee took effect. "It'll make it easier. Or at least more pleasant. I could have prosecuted her without that, but this'll be better."

"Did she say anything else?" I asked.

"Beyond what she said to you?" Lou shook her head. "She confessed to killing her sister. She told me why. Frenetta was thinking of selling the B and B, and Vonnie didn't want her to. Her main concern was with Chip and Nina's father, the developer. She didn't realize a deal had already been worked out with someone else."

She glanced at Gloria and Hildy. "So she put some of Groot's sleeping medicine in Frenetta's wine, and waited until Frenetta went upstairs to her apartment. Then she knocked on the door, ostensibly to talk about it again, and when Frenetta said it was too late, Vonnie got angry. Frenetta acted groggy, Vonnie helped her to bed. And killed her."

There was a pause, while we all digested this.

"She didn't seem upset," Lou added. "No remorse that I could see. It was all about the house. And about their mother, who left the house to Frenetta and not her. That was really all she talked about."

There was another pause.

"What about the husband?" Rafe muttered.

Lou glanced at him. "Says he didn't know she was going to do it. Says he didn't know she did it until the next morning, when y'all went up to the apartment and found her dead. I have no way to know whether he's lying or telling the truth."

"Could go either way," I said.

She nodded. "I'm not sure it matters. Vonnie killed her. Whether Groot knew or not, he's being punished. His wife will spend the rest of her life in prison."

"I guess there's no chance she'll plead not guilty."

Lou shook her head. "Not with a confession on record. And that's what'll make it easier. No trial. She'll go before the judge in a couple of days and get sentenced, and that'll be it."

"Convenient." And cheap. She wouldn't need attorney fees if there was no trial. So much for my reassurance to Gloria and Hildy that Vonnie would need all the money she could scrape together to defend herself.

The two of them exchanged a glance. "We have the contract," Gloria said.

Hildy nodded.

Lou looked from one to the other of them, and then decided to leave well enough alone. She turned to me. "Y'all headed back to Nashville?"

"We were just talking about that," I said. "And I think I'd like to, if it's all right with you. This hasn't exactly been the honeymoon of my dreams."

"The sex was good," Rafe muttered.

We all turned to stare at him, and he must have realized it because he blinked. "What did I say?"

"That the sex was good," I told him. At least it had sounded like that.

"Oh." He thought for a second. "It was. But I was talking about the beach. The beach was good."

"Do you want to go on the beach again before we go home? We can spare a couple hours before we head out." We'd still make it home by tonight. I figured I'd be doing most of the driving, since he could barely keep his head up.

He shook his head. "Nah. I just wanna sleep."

"You can sleep all the way home. I'll get you there in one piece."

It was a testament to how tired he was that all he did was nod. Normally, he would have fought me for the privilege of driving.

"Sheriff?" I turned to Lou.

She waved a hand. "Go on. Take care of yourselves. Stop by if you're ever back in Davenport."

I said we would.

"And don't speed on your way out of town."

"I wouldn't dream of it," I said, and turned to Rafe. "Ready?"

He nodded blearily, and pushed to his feet. I'd already put the bags in the car, so we were all set.

"Come back and see us," Hildy said, walking us to the back door like a proper hostess, while Gloria continued to entertain— or quiz—the sheriff in the dining room. "I have a good feeling about this. We'll be here next summer."

She smiled.

"We'll remember that," I told her.

She watched while I maneuvered Rafe into the passenger seat, and moved the seat back so his legs—much longer than mine—had enough room to stretch. Then I headed around the car to the driver's side door. "It was nice to meet you both. Good luck with everything."

"Safe travels," Hildy said, and waved as I drove out of the parking lot, away from the Victorian house, and the garage apartment, and the crime scene tape strung across the stairway.

When I could no longer see the place in my rearview mirror, I glanced at Rafe. "Still awake?"

He mumbled something.

"Want me to stop on the way out of town so you can splash in the water one last time before we go?"

He shook his head. "Take me home." He didn't even open his eyes.

"As you wish," I said, and stepped on the gas.

# # #

ABOUT THE AUTHOR

New York Times and *USA Today* bestselling author Jenna Bennett (Jennie Bentley) writes the Do It Yourself home renovation mysteries for Berkley Prime Crime and the Savannah Martin real estate mysteries for her own gratification. She also writes a variety of romance for a change of pace. Originally from Norway, she has spent more than twenty five years in the US, and still hasn't been able to kick her native accent.

For more information, please visit Jenna's website:
www.JennaBennett.com

Made in the USA
Las Vegas, NV
02 November 2024

10732387R00069